SPACE Between Us

If this isn't the story of my Multiverse

SHYRA VISHNOI

notionpress.com

INDIA • SINGAPORE • MALAYSIA

ISBN

Hardcase 979-8-89556-950-4
Paperback 979-8-89519-830-8

If betrayal was forgivable,
Even Satan would have been residing next to God in Heaven.

To my Brother,
Who fought against the society with me.

Playlist

Heartbroken as I was, I needed these songs.

Into it - Chase Atlantic
This is what heartbreak feels like - JVKE.
I see Red - Everybody Loves an Outlaw
Lost in Japan, Shawn Mendes
Reminder - The Weeknd
Somebody that I used to know - Gotye, Kimbra
Lost- Maroon 5
Sad girl, Lana Del Ray
Devil in Disguise, AP
Strawberries and Cigarettes, Troye Sivan
Creepin' - Metro Boomin, The Weeknd, & 21 Savage
Summertime Sadness, Lana Del Ray
You and I dancing in the moonlight, Kim Jennie
Boyfriend, Dove Cameron
Starboy - The Weeknd
Lonely - Akon

Song that was playing at the back of the fashion show,
NASTY, Zeina

Contents

Contents

Chapter 1

Hades

It had been two fucking years since I met her right around this time of the year. She and I have totally different perspectives of the world. Still, I find myself most compatible with her.

She is my best friend.

My mood wasn't very delightful at present, so I came to the library to find her. As soon as I entered the door, I saw her indulged in some books with ear dopes stuffed into both her ears and not giving a care about her surroundings, her hair tied up and a pair of nerdy glasses. *She looks beautiful.*

I paced to her and met eyes with her. *God, her eyes are like a mirror. I get so sweaty when I look too deep into them.*

She saw me.

Those emerald eyes always look into the soul of the people, and those light crimson lake, soft pouty lips of hers make a lot of people spill their deepest, darkest secrets.

Heather Kades is the one and only in the whole universe.

She was also named by the seniors the gossip queen, last summer, and she never degrades her tag because she knows everyone's business, everyone's tea, but doesn't care about anyone (except it doesn't include me or her few closest people).

I banged my phone on the table while seating myself in front of her. The sound of the banging from the phone made her ticked off. "Looking at the phone screen right now, I guess someone is in a bad mood," she taunted. Eyebrows notched, she took a sip of her cranberry juice and said, "Shall I ask, or are you going to spill it yourself?"

"My dad is giving me a Mercedes."

"Ohhh, and I just want a million dollars," came the mocking reply. I can't believe how I was handling this bitch for two years who still tried to mirror every line she could from F.R.I.E.N.D.S.

"At least hear the full story. I will get the Mercedes if I move back home to Greece after senior year and help my father in business."

"So where is the problem?" she asked as if she didn't care. I would leave, and I felt at that moment how could a person possibly be that dumb. Judging from mood, couldn't she figure it out herself that I don't want to leave.

"The problem is that I don't want to leave Los Angeles."

"Why?"

"Because everything I want is here. You, my friends, among other things," I replied.

She rose and asked me to help her put the books back on from where she picked them up.

As soon as we finished half of those, my hands were still occupied holding a lot of them, and I was still telling her about the deal my father made, "ouch, that hurts" - she just flicked me, "Why did you do that?"

"To check, if you have a brain?" she taunted.

"Did you find it?"

"Negative."

Hell, yeah, she is a mean ass, "Why do you say so?"

"Because it's obvious you are not thinking straight. You should go and handle your father's business and help him with stuff," she placed a hand on my arm and continued, "He needs you, and you are here with us for one more year. I'll keep visiting you. Plus, Delilah is going to Greece too. Might as well see both my best friends there."

"Are you sure?" I asked.

"Three thousand percent. You will get the Mercedes too, and soon I'll be the one taking it for a spin."

"Ohh like I would trust you with it. I won't give you a cycle to ride on and here you are talking about driving the car." I don't think it's a request expression took over her face.

I didn't promise her that I will go back to Greece, so I just played along and nodded my head like I understood the point she just made.

I didn't want to leave her nor my homies. I had lived in Los Angeles for seven years, and that was the only home I had known for so long, and the home Heather built here. I don't want to leave it, and I never will.

After building a strong conversation, we both left for a break and went down to the cafeteria where we found nearly all our friends sitting together, which was pretty common as we all hung out together at this time.

"Oh my Gawd! Lovebirds are here." Delilah squinted and shouted in a voice loud enough for the floors above to hear us.

"Shut the fuck up. If anyone hears, everyone will think that we are dating. Delilah Maseque, one day you are going to be my death for sure." Heather placed her belongings on the table and told me to bring her some food. She seated herself on the chair beside Delilah.

By the time I got myself back with a tray of food in my hand and a cranberry juice in another, they were already in a casual conversation. "Thank you so much, Hades." the warmth in her green gaze filled me up like the sun warms up an entire field of maize.

"Great! Now I don't have a seat," I announced to the entire party sitting there.

"Don't be so dramatic. Get yourself a chair, or is it your ego that is pushing too hard to get it?" This bitch won't stop humiliating me. No matter how much I tell her to stop passing comments on my ego, but she won't cut it out.

I smirked out of nowhere like an idiot to show that her words didn't just burn me. As for my ego, I pushed it too hard to pick up her cranberry juice, so I did. Of course, a curse left from her mouth because she knew that I know she loves this damn juice a lot.

"Okay, sorry. Cut it out and give me back the juice."

"I am sorry too, Alpha. If you want the juice, come and get it yourself," I said. I moved a step backwards, and she elevated from her seat to take the drink, which she absolutely loves.

"You are such a child," she complained.

I swung my arm up to reassure the possibility that she can't get it. In front of a five-feet-four girl, I am a beast. No way in hell could she reach up to it. "Well, you can't seem to reach for your cranberry juice and snatch it from the child." I mocked her on her being the shortest one.

"Aren't you an asshole!" she narrowed her eyes to show she meant it, for real this time.

After trying for five minutes and failing miserably to get to the cup from my hand, I finally gave it to her. While she was amazed by it and made herself busy using her pouty lips to suck the juice all from the straw. In the meantime, I took the seat that she left.

"Aww, looks like the seat is mine now." I mocked again.

She shook her head, a little, telling me the same thing about being immature.

I didn't give much crap about it, but as soon as she turned away to get herself a seat, I grabbed her from her wrist and yanked her onto my lap. "What The Fuck, Hades."

"You can sit here. It's comfortable, you know." I notched my left eyebrow. She isn't the type of shy person, so she played along. Definitely, if someone saw my hands wrapped around her waist and her arm around my shoulder, they will establish us as a couple.

As I held her close to me, I felt her fragrance devouring my soul.

She smells like strawberries and vanilla. I hope she tastes like them too.

We engage ourselves in normal gossip when we heard a cell ringtone. We all checked our cells, but it was Delilah's which was ringing.

She excused herself out and soon came back. Out of curiosity, I asked her about the call. She turned her face to Heather and said, "Mom called, Heather. I guess there's been a little damage to our portrait while moving out some stuff, so she asked us back home immediately. Let me grab my bag from the locker, and you bring the car out by the gate."

"Yeah. Okay," Heather replied. She looked at me and stood up. "I gotta go, sweethearts. Meet you guys at the party on Saturday." She paused while packing her belongings that she rested on the table. "Hades, help me with this stuff to carry out to the car." I did exactly what she told me to.

As we walked out of the cafeteria with her heavy books in my hand, I gathered up the courage to question her about one thing I had been meaning to ask her for so long. "Delilah isn't your sibling. She is your best friend, right?" she nodded, "but then why does she call your mother, mom."

"Delilah and I have been inseparable for as long as I could remember. Our mothers were best friends before us even being born, but life isn't always that happy."

Her voice sounded low, like she knows the pain. "We were only a couple of seven-year-olds when we were cycling, and we went back inside the house and heard the news of a car crash. Two pairs of eyes were already set on the television. It wasn't mine and Delilah's; it was my parents.' My mother saw us and immediately hugged her, her eyes filled with tears. That's the time we both realised the car that crashed was her parents.' My mom not only took her in but also established that she has two daughters."

She took a long sigh. "She didn't cry or say anything for three days straight, and for even one second, I didn't leave her side, thinking she'll cry and I won't be there for her. On the fifth day, she let her pain out through her eyes, exhausting herself for three hours and finally landed on my lap to sleep. I held her tight, and I slept too. Since that day till now, she calls my mother 'mom' too because-" her voice changed into a dramatic one. "Morriaana Kades considers herself Delilah's mother too."

I could watch Heather's eyes going dim and swelling up, water, and a smile that is trying to conceal her pain that she had kept hidden for so long. I held my arms around her shoulder to comfort her. "I am so sorry. I didn't know that Delilah went through so much."

"Yeah, she is a strong girl."

As soon as we reached the car, I placed the belongings on the backseat, and Delilah came soon after.

I closed the door of the car and told her to give me a call when she reaches home or leave a text instead. She waved and drove off the school campus.

Chapter 2
Heather

"Delilah, will you come out here, baby, and help me with these boxes," my mom shouted from downstairs.

"Yeah, I'll be down there in a minute," Delilah replied from the room to mom while tossing my stuff angrily. "Why do we have to move?" she complained. "I don't want to miss the smell of mom's breakfast every morning. I don't want to leave this house. Dad is not going to be there every Friday evening showing up at the door with desserts."

"You are just being melodramatic, honey. We are like ten minutes away from the house. Don't worry about the desserts, too; we are going to visit on weekends." As soon as those words showed up from my side, she felt at a little ease.

She went downstairs to help mom, while I decided to pack her desk because she was never planning to do. My eyes widened just looking at the mess. Pencil shavings on the table rather than in the dustbin, no heading written on the papers, and wrappers of food covered approximately half of the table.

I took a deep breath and opened that one drawer, and it was more of a mess than I had ever seen. It didn't surprise me because the drawer clutter was much more. Chocolates and more than chocolates were there, wrappers, paints, her money, credit cards – in fact, were just lying there amidst all this.

At that moment, I pitied myself because I had made the decision to pack her desk all by myself.

I observed the drawer in order to clean, and I found three books lying with Calligraphy, covered with fancy paper and a year marked on them. IT WAS A DIARY. It wasn't just a diary; it was Delilah's year diary. I flipped through a few pages of the 2019 diary and saw photos of me and Delilah sticking.

Nostalgia hit me hard.

I was going to open twenty-twenty year's diary, but I heard a mumbling besides the footsteps of Delilah on the stairs, so I picked up those diaries and placed them under the quilt of the bed.

"I still can't understand why we have to move," she complained again while walking up the stairs.

"Because we are going to be adults soon, and don't you think we should take the burden on ourselves now? Plus, we will have all the privacy, you know. It's five blocks away. You can visit mom anytime you want, but I want you to be my roommate. Despite the fact that you are irritating, I couldn't think of anyone as my roommate but you," I explained.

She nodded in agreement.

Time to explode the bomb, I thought to myself and finally flipped the quilt on the other side, showcasing the diaries. Clicked my nails on them and drew her attention, "Care to elaborate what these are?"

I guess she just died from the shock. She held on, her gaze widened with those brown eyes, like the next thing she was going to do was murder me. Finally, some words left her lips, "You gotta be fucking kidding me right now."

She tangled me onto the bed, but I never surrendered to giving the diaries to her until she told me what these were exactly and why she stopped writing after twenty-twenty-one. She just sits on top of me, and hell yeah, she is heavy. "Damn, you weigh a tonne, bitch. Okay, okay, I will give you these diaries only when you tell me what you wrote in them." I guess it sounded convincing because it got her thinking, "Can you please get off my back now!"

She got off me and told me about the contents as soon as I gave her the diaries. She also told me about the pictures I saw. Further, she explained that she forgot about those until today and didn't have time to start with the twenty-twenty-two diary when I asked about it.

"Maybe you like this one." She held out the twenty-twenty diary and gave it to me.

"Why are you giving me this? These are your honey," I replied.

"You told me that nostalgia hit hard when you saw our pre-puberty pictures, so consider it a present. It has everything about you and Hades. Everything! From the moment you guys met until you guys became best friends."

My expression changed from a smile to a disgusted one, "Why, in the first place, did you write about us in your diary?"

"I am going to be honest here. I was really jealous at first of Hades. I thought he was going to steal my one and only best friend, but more than that, I was really excited that you were finally open to making other friends besides me, so that's why I wrote about him and you."

My eyes, with comfort in them, forced me to hug her. I rested my head on her shoulder and wrapped my hands around her. "I ain't gonna leave you, honey, no matter what comes and goes," I assured her.

It's past dinner time in our new apartment. Now that Delilah and I have separate beds, she went to sleep immediately because she was tired from moving all day. I look around finding boxes lying and sense a peace on being left alone.

The apartment wasn't big enough, but for two people, it was larger. For two people, there were three bedrooms, each with a bathroom attached. Since Delilah and I took one each, we decided to either make the third room a guest room or convert it into a game room, depending on the circumstances.

I walked out on the balcony, which was connected to every room. We lived on the ninth floor, and I experienced a heaven on Earth when I saw the amazing view outside. It was absolutely ravishing, something that I couldn't even comprehend in my own mind.

I took a quick stroll, but I had to move back into the room since all the windy weather was really giving me chills. My room was on the left side from the entrance gate, far enough from Delilah's room, but I could still hear her snoring like a pig even though I had closed the door of my room.

The privacy, the peace. I was undergoing, instantly got my lips curved in a smile. My bedroom wasn't decorated yet, but still, it had only a king-size bed, and my clothes were all that I had in my closet. *And Delilah's diary.*

I sat myself on the bed and opened her diary, with the first page welcoming me with photos of her and me. It was us, a couple of eleven-year-olds in the painting class, spilling colours on each other's clothes and faces. A sigh left my mouth, thinking that all these years she had kept it. Safely.

I flipped the page and saw the entry directly in April. I turned over a few, and the diary wasn't in continuous dates. These were all written whenever Delilah either felt left out or when she was sad.

27th April 2020,
Wednesday.

Oh, my gawdd, where do I even start? Heather is still stuck on that worthless boy, Chris. Chris has been the only one she loved truly since fourth class, but he turned out to be an asshole as well; he got her hurt many times. She can never move on from that silly crush of hers if she doesn't explore, but the weirdest thing happened today.

We both volunteered for the basketball team today at the match, and I see a lot of girls wandering around this boy who has a height of approximately six feet above inches and a muscled body. I have seen him before; he was of the same age, but I couldn't get hold of his name. I asked Heather about him, but she had no idea.

A voice from the back shouted to him as Captain, and his head snapped when I figured out who he was.

It was Hades Hawthorne, the sole descendant of Atlantis. Atlantis had been the only legal business operating in international waters. Well, of course, it is! It's the only company that has casino ships and cruises in the ocean with a permit. He has been transferred to this school and has been here for the last 5 years.

He never really cared to attend the classes before, but today something unexpected happened when I saw him in our English class. He came and sat directly behind Heather. I saw him whisper something, but as politely as ever, Heather turned her face and told him no and thank you.

When the period bell rang, she walked out of the class immediately, and Hades and his friends gathered around me soon after. Hades told me how he broke up with his long-distance girlfriend and finally found a girl to replace her.

I had to tell him about Chris, so I did, and another disappointment flashed over his face, but he didn't let me go to my other class until I gave him her social media info.

Is she writing for me or against me? She told me that I would be having fun reading this, but swear to God, from what I have read by now, it seems she hates me and probably bitches about me in her diaries.

It was only the first page, and she already made me a certified prude.

I heard a buzz sound in my phone. I picked it up to check it and found Hades' message flash on the screen. I double-tapped to open.

Hades: Are you awake?

He uses a lot of abbreviations, no doubt.

Me: yeah. Why?

Hades: Can't you sleep, thinking of me?? *Smirk emoji*

Me: You really think highly of yourself. *Unamused emoji*

Hades: I think highly of myself because I have the capability to pull an all-nighter.

Me: You really text me at one in the morning to flex your skills.

Me: I don't have time for this. Imma sleep now. Good night!! *Sleep emoji*

I placed the phone back in its original place and flipped the page of the diary.

29ᵗʰ April 2020,
Wednesday.

I've told Heather a million times not to do a job, but she never listens. Despite the fact that the mall she works in is owned by her father, she still likes to work at a small cosmetic centre, which is a part of it. She didn't care who would see her until today when Hades stopped by the shop, and she eventually went into trauma. Hades' friends and I were watching from a corner when he asked her out. In a few minutes, I saw the dumbest move, or I thought it was when Hades slammed cash on the counter and bought all the cosmetics. One by one, his driver and guards took all the shopping bags.

He literally emptied her store.

Soon after, he joined us, and I asked him what happened when he showed all of us a one-dollar buck with Heather's number written on it. He further told us that Heather challenged him to buy her time, and he bought the whole store for her just so she could get some time off with him.

They both love challenges. It's weird how similar they both were.

The actual surprise was when we reached home and saw lined-up boxes and bags from her store with cosmetics in them. A note was written on the biggest one.

<u>This is for you, Alpha. Don't take it back to the store, but keep it as a present.</u>

I saw her with a smirk on her lips, and I know she will go on a date with him, so I will take the charge to decide her outfit.

I like Hades for Heather, but if she rejects him, she'll surely be the dumbest bitch. What Hades had done is something I guess no man will ever do, just to buy some time for a girl he barely knows or consider the possibility that he will be rejected.

I read these two entries picturing a flashback of how this all started. If it wouldn't have been me volunteering for that basketball team, I would have never met Hades.

I knew how this story was going to go down, but I didn't want to stop reading. However, it was late, and I had an early call, so I turned off the bed lamp on the nightstand and slipped the duvet above me while sinking into every moment I had felt.

Chapter 3

Hades

I planned to cancel the rager or birthday party, whatever the hell this was. Heather blackmailed me into joining it; otherwise, I would end up with a knife in my chest.

Only because of her I took out the last-minute outfit I could. I decided to go with black jeans and a skin-fitted black t-shirt to flex the muscles. For an extra touch, I wore a checked black and white H&M shirt and left it unbuttoned. My cross pendant was necessary because my look wouldn't be complete without it, and I was still looking damn dashing in it. Couldn't help myself.

I walked inside the house from the main gate, and it was freaking huge. Not that my penthouse was any smaller, and my real home in Greece was bigger than this, but I never showed it off like this.

The infinity pool on the main lawn had half of the people being naked and going skinny dipping.

I looked around to discover Heather in my eye-line but couldn't seem to find her. I called her multiple times, shot her texts, and then laid my eyes on Delilah.

I knew she wasn't alone, but I still made my pace to her. She was surrounded by the people of our friends, and Heather wasn't to be seen anywhere.

"Where is Heather? I can't get hold of her either on text or call," I said.

"She isn't joining!" she responded.

A familiar voice followed, "Why are you so worked up about it?" My head snapped when I saw Joshua make a taunt, implying that I might be in love with her or something. But who am I to correct the guy (that we are just best friends) who believed love was stupid when you can get laid?

I understood that in my first relationship in sophomore year if it hadn't been for that girl, I would have never met Heather.

"She, herself, first blackmailed me into coming, and now she isn't joining herself," I replied to his curiosity.

I told Delilah to follow me into the kitchen and help with the drinks, "Where is she?"

I see the hesitation - "She isn't well." My heart raced, *is she sick? Did something happen to her? Why didn't she call?*

"Anything serious?" Wondering all the questions and possibilities.

"Nah, just, you know." She pulled me closer to her neck by grabbing my collar and whispered, "She is on her period." She released, and I sensed pity glaring in her eyes when she added, "The first two days are unbearable. Despite the fact she took the pill to join this party, the pain never left; therefore, she decided to stay at home."

"Oh," before I could reply with any other words, a message came through from Heather when I felt the vibrations of my phone on my hand.

Heather: Sorry I couldn't join the party. Too unwell to do so. Enjoy and have fun.

I looked at those words for plenty of time when Joshua shouted from the bean bag he was sitting on, "Hey, man! Care to join?"

"Actually, some work lined up. I've got to go," Delilah said as she walked back to the group and shot me a look as if she knew where I was heading.

I went outside and started the engine of my car. I drove off at speed.

I knew that Delilah had the idea of where I was going, therefore, she sent the address immediately as I left the party. She was a kind of blessing to me and Heather both. If it wasn't for her telling me ways to impress Heather in the beginning, I might never have had a best friend as such.

I reached her place and took the elevator up. It was an old, classic building, and she lived on the ninth floor.

The first five floors had four apartments each, whereas the next five had two apartments each. The building only went up to the tenth floor, and she still chose the ninth floor.

I got all this in the first week of their shifting since Heather had no other topic other than her new apartment. She was genuinely happy about that move as she took one step forward to become an adult.

The elevator was too small for me, I thought, and a hundred red lilies - which are customised because she likes the colour red - in my hands. I walked to the first apartment, and the nameplate captured my attention.

Delilah & Heather's
901

I knocked on the door, and there she was, in a high ponytail, standing right in front of me in red thigh-high shorts and an oversized black t-shirt bearing her shoulder. Slippers on her feet and sweat running down from her forehead to her chin.

No make-up whatsoever, and she still managed to take my breath away.

Her emerald eyes, as always, expanded unexpectedly when she saw me leaning on her door frame. I could sense that she was shocked to the core, and I felt like my heart was about to jump out of my throat.

"What are you doing here?" she sounded confused.

"I couldn't stand the party alone, so I came here to chill with you. What are you doing anyway?" I knew why she was here, but I still wanted to check if she thought of me as close enough to share her problems.

"I was unpacking the sealed boxes." She took a pause as my eyes lingered over to the sealed boxes behind her. "You shouldn't waste your weekend like this."

"As long as I am with you, I am not wasting my weekend. Now that I have come all the way, let me help you," I handed her the red lilies. "By the way, these are for you and your new apartment."

"Well, thank you for these." She took the bouquet from my hand and opened the door wide to welcome me. "Make yourself at home."

For one hour, I helped her unpack the boxes. We found some really weird stuff, and most of it was Delilah's. After some work, we finally sat down on the couch. Heather literally pushed a desk in such a condition that I could just put my leg up on the centre table.

"So, how's the pain?" I finally gathered up the courage and asked her.

"She told you, didn't she?" Looking at her murderous expression, I pray for Delilah's life right now. "Well, it's fine now." Rolling her eyes, she replied.

"Do you want to go out and eat something?" I asked before anything awkward began.

"Let's order in. I am not in any position to go out." She pointed out, looking at her clothes.

"It doesn't matter. I will be there to protect you." Her lips curved into a smile, confirming a decision. "Okay. Let's go then."

We walked out of the apartment, and she locked the door behind me. I pushed the button to the ground floor in the elevator, and she handed over the apartment keys to the receptionist, giving her instructions to give them to Delilah in case she came home.

We reached outside, and she saw my car, "You got a new one?"

"You bet I did!"

"Why?" shock spiralled through her.

"Just a new model." It was a red Chevrolet Corvette ZR1. I only bought it in red colour because she loved that colour. As she seated herself, the car was filled with the fragrance she was emitting.

"Oh, Saucy," she said, looking at the interior of the car. I got it redecorated with certain lights to shine the classiest interior. I started the engine when she leaned over to my shoulder, and her puppy emerald eyes looked at me, "Can I drive?"

My urge was pushing me to say yes, but my mouth had different opinions. "Absolutely not." Her face changed expressions like a person changing metros. Looking at her right now, it looked like she had swallowed a smoke train.

I kept driving, and all I wanted to see was Heather right now instead of the road in front of me.

I wanted to grab her and tell her that she was the reason I hadn't dated anyone for the last two years. Even though on our first date she told me everything about Chris, she also knew that I wouldn't mind that guy, but she didn't want to give us a chance until she gained feelings. Fair of her to ask.

Every day, I was trying a little harder than my best. That's why, after her sweet rejection, I asked her to be my friend so I could get to know more about her and spend more time with her. Soon after, she addressed me as her best friend, but from my perspective, I always wanted to be more than that to her.

In the state she was in, I guess the best food she could have was street food, so I made a stop at the street stall since she liked street food A LOT. It really didn't matter to her where she was eating as long as the food was to her taste. "Here we are," I said while stopping the car in front of the food truck.

"Oh, street food," she said. "Can we eat an ice cream too?"

We both got out of the car, "I don't have a problem in giving you an ice cream, but I don't think you should eat it while you are on your chums," I protested while walking towards the vendor.

Without saying anything, she took the seat where she could find one. I went back to the vendor and gave him the order.

As soon as I placed the food and beers in front of her, she crossed her legs, giving a perfect view of her thick thighs, and looked me in the eye. "Why?"

"Why what?"

"Why can't I eat an ice cream on my period?" she sounded so genuine of not knowing some obvious things that women should be aware of. Especially the ones that goes through a lot of pain and yet her question was so stupid for me.

"You don't know?"

"What?" She didn't know about it, and it kinda got me surprised, but it feels weirder to even tell. For her future safety, I had to let her know.

"That if girls were on their chums eats, chilled food, or you know, icy things." I took my time to complete my words and put them in a more elegant way, but her obvious reaction finally helped me to spill whatever I had in my mind, "The channel gets swelled up an-"

"Eww! Eww! Eww!" she covered her ears with both hands and a disgusting face she made right after. "I don't wanna know that and WHY DO YOU KNOW THIS?"

"You should have thought that before asking me, and I have a sister. I am the younger one, so she used to tell me ways to prevent her pain."

"So, you are your sister's boy." Well, she knows how to hurt my ego.

"I hate to say this, but yep. I love her, and she loves me too. The fact that we didn't have anybody but each other is a bond none of us can ever break." I took a sip of my drink, and she repeated my actions, "By the way, if we are talking about my sister, I have been meaning to ask you this: my sister's wedding is coming up, and I want you to join me."

A chuckle left her mouth, sprinkling beer on the food, but then I gave her a dead serious look about what I asked. "Are you sure? It's your family function, Hades," she tried to explain to me the consequences of bringing a girl home.

I listened to her, EVERY WORD, carefully while finishing my fourth beer, and she was still on her second. "Alpha, it's either with you or with no one. So, you coming?"

"I will have to ask my parents, but I don't think they will say no. So, yeah, I guess." I smiled for obvious reasons. She was coming with me to my home. Never have I ever imagined bringing a girl home, knowing how my family would react, but I knew she could handle them, "Where is it anyway?"

"Don't worry. I'll text you the details."

After eating, I told her to sit back in the car, and I planned to drop her off at the apartment.

By the time we got there, I saw Heather sleeping at my side. I walked out of the car to the other side and removed the seat belt while sliding one arm around her waist and the other on her nape. I looked down at her and realised that she had fallen into a deep sleep during the twenty-minute ride.

I walked inside the main entrance to the building's lobby and took the elevator.

I was in the elevator and glanced at every feature of her, which made me feel the way I shouldn't feel for her. I knew my insights. She was more than a friend to me, but if I confessed and she didn't return it, it would only make us grow apart.

I rang the doorbell of her house with my elbow. She was still fast asleep. Delilah opened the door, and before greeting her, my eyes fell on her, covered in a bed sheet. "You are having sex," I implied.

"Well, I was having sex," she corrected me, and to my shock, she reminded me, "and Shushh, she is asleep."

"So, open the door wide so I can slide her onto the bed," I whispered.

She opened the door, vast, and I went directly into Heather's bedroom and slipped her inside the quilt. I leaned down to stroke her hair and sent my goodbye to her with a kiss on her neck.

It was my favourite part of her body yet. My urge had been pushing me all night, but No.

That was my limit.

I turned around to leave and saw Delilah leaning on her bedroom door, finally with a night suit on, and said, "You sure you guys are just best friends?"

"She only likes me as her best friend," I stated.

She pressed her lips, indicating a very similar look I had seen before, as if she didn't believe me. She walked two steps forward, looked up at me, and said, "But do you only like her as a friend, or was what I just saw something more?"

"Apparently, we are just friends. That's all you need to know," I confirmed.

Her eyebrows lifted as her head shook, looking down, knowing I would say something like that. "Sure. Whatever you say," she taunted.

Chapter 4

Heather

I woke up earlier than usual, and I guess the hangover was hitting me hard. Not that I drank much, but beer is one of my weaknesses. I saw the time on the clock hanging against the wall, and it was four in the morning.

I knew how I ended up in my bed. I felt the weight of the stare Hades had on me in the elevator, and the kiss on my neck took me to a whole new level. I know I should not feel that way, but to be honest, it's the first time I'm feeling euphoric.

I had always thought of Hades as my comfort person. A person I knew would never leave me, but every brush of his fingers, every touch, every word he spoke got me into his spell as I had never felt during Chris. This was the first time I experienced my heartbeat racing more than I had ever done with Chris.

I got off my bed and moved to the kitchen to get myself a snack. I opened the top drawer, grabbed the box of Pringles and a few chocolates, and laid back on the bed again. Furthermore, I opened my side drawer and took out Delilah's diary to read.

It was the only way to get my heart to stop blushing at the bare minimum. I flipped through the first few pages, which I had already read, and turned directly to the starting month of May.

2nd May 2020,
Saturday.

She returned three hours ago from the date and slipped into her shorts and oversized t-shirt immediately, replacing that jet black pants and vest of hers, giving her a perfect hourglass figure. Obviously, I advised her to go with dresses, but she wanted to show off her women empowerment side.

She didn't speak to me about anything, but she went to bed immediately. I assumed something must have not worked out. I am surprised that the group chat is dead. Hades invited me right after she agreed to go on a date with him. He kept texting how he was going to make her fall in love, but it's been three hours since she returned and still no news.

I just ended my call with Hades. He called me an hour ago and filled me up with every detail of their date. Let's start with the fact that he took her on a cycling date. Not only did they cycle in the city forest, but they also discussed many things while cycling. Later, he took her to a famous Italian restaurant, where she mentioned that she liked Italian food.

He is extremely rich, and still, he played the most normal date to make her comfortable. After their meal, he and Heather took a long stroll in the nearby park.

Everything was going great until the end when he leaned in, and she pressed his chest with her hand, telling him that she felt a spark between them. But she still doesn't want to admit the truth that she might still be in love with Chris. Not just LIKE, but she actually mentioned the word LOVE.

I wish she were awake right now so I could slap her across her face and get her into the sense that 'don't let go of this guy for some asshole you ridiculously believe yourself to be in love with.' Today, I kinda respect Hades for respecting her decision. We all know he doesn't want to let go of her, so he did the unbelievable - he asked her to be his friend. Even though I thought it was stupid, I also think it was sweet of him to do so.

Chapter 5

Hades

I saw Heather sitting on the stairs of the school ground. Her eyes were focused on the footballers. It kind of got me to think that we, were just a few steps away on the side, but she still chose to sit alone rather than joining us.

Is she thinking about something or someone I don't know of? Or is she into footballers? She has always been so mysterious for me to crack. Around me, I saw members of my group making a conversation about something that I consider pure noise and nothing else.

The background fades automatically when my eyes fall on her. She was like the south to my north. Her eyes had been the only eyes I wanted to drown myself into.

I snapped myself out of the freakish imagination and watched, her sitting there all by herself with her cell phone. I looked at her more closely with an aim of her noticing me, but she was too lost in her own world, her own peace.

"I'll be back," I announced to my group.

I strive to approach her, and that's when I noticed Air Pods stuffed in her ear. *She had been listening to songs; that's why she didn't even raise her head for a glance.* She started listening to songs when she felt lonely or left out. She used to believe in fairy tale endings, but when the outcome of her love story didn't show as she deserved, she changed her perception. Fair of her to do so.

Still, my steps never stopped until I took my seat beside her, touching shoulders with her, and took one air pod from her ear. She looked at me in wonder, "What the fu-."

It was the middle of the song, just as soon as I realised it was 'you and me dancing in the moonlight' from Jennie Kim, whom she used to admire. I have heard her playlist many times, but this song was never in it. However, she used to listen to it on repeat. It was soothing for her, bringing her peace, I guess.

I placed a finger on her lips and muttered, "Shhh, I am listening to your song." My finger felt numb instantly because her lips were so soft. My heartbeat took on an engine, and I took a deep breath.

I waited until the song finished playing and told her to hand me the phone to make her listen to one of my favourites. "You have terrible taste in music," she said, "if you are putting something, put something good that will not bleed my ears, for God's sake." With a stingy look, she gave me an order. I took it as a challenge.

I played 'Lost in Japan' by Shawn Mendes. I knew it was a song that she would never remove. It really doesn't count in my preferences, yet I hit the play button on Apple Music.

"Aren't you going to say something about my taste in music?" I mocked.

She shook her head, "No. It's perfect." She looked at me, and I looked at her. Before knowing anything, I put my head onto her shoulders, and she froze. It took her a few minutes to be back on Earth and be subtle, "One day, I will go to his concert for real."

"I'll take you. I promise," I said.

"Why promise this thing?"

"Because it matters to you."

I heard the period bell, and I left her shoulder when I told her I had to leave for my practice, "Meet you tomorrow."

"Yeah," she muttered.

Heather

I was sitting alone on the stairs at the field before Hades disturbed me, with his captivating presence. I was only there to avoid him and to distract myself from watching him, but he surely didn't like the idea of me being alone without him.

I was listening to songs, feeling confused. I had encountered what Hades did just to make me smile and take away the pain of the period I had been enduring about four days ago. He asked me to join him at his sister's wedding.

Is it only me who can sense the tension, or can he, too? Was it really him flirting in the car, or did I just imagine it because I wanted that?

I knew he could.

When he rested his head on my shoulder, I could practically feel his heartbeat. My heart wasn't anywhere behind because it was racing to reach cloud nine.

My head snappe at the voice that reached me. It was Delilah. "Where have you been?" she asked, completing her breath. "I was looking everywhere for you."

"Why were you looking everywhere for me?"

"You're going home right now, " she ordered.

"Why?"

"Because I don't want to study anymore." Classic Delilah. She leaves the school premises whenever she doesn't want to sit in her classes anymore. Never bothered about her future when she was already going to Greece with the scholarship she always wanted.

"Okay." I stood up and handed her my bag. She was actually thinking I was going to say no, but what comes out of my mouth surprised her, "Then we are going home." I was tired as well from all the overthinking, and I guess I need some time off of it.

Chapter 6
Heather

Another day, I was sitting in the cafeteria, drinking cranberry juice and eating bubble gum. I didn't know where Hades was, but I did know that Joshua got stood up on his date just now. It was so funny that he missed school, got his hair done, and cancelled his plans only to be stood up.

"You seriously think my misery is funny to you," I heard Joshua complaining to me over a call.

"Well, I know you like her, but she didn't show up, so-" I gotta show him the reality, "it basically means you got stood up," a big smile appeared on my face as I completed.

For the next fifteen minutes, I kept on making jokes about everyone who stood up, and he took it all in. "Laugh all you want, babe, but you know I'll be the one making jokes."

"What are you going to joke about me?"

"I guess your low self-esteem." He knew that after Chris, I was so insecure about my body. I never liked to be the one in the limelight, and still, I was one of the famous entities because of Hades.

"You bitch."

My phone slipped from my ear. It was pulled by someone from the back.

I spun around to see who it was, and my eyes landed directly on Hades. "She's gotta go. Bye." He hung up the call.

"Hey," I protested while my hands flew in the air for a gesture. "You have no right to do that!"

He rested a finger above my lips. "Shut the hell up and listen, Alpha."

As my eyes were fixated on him, I saw him seating himself down on the chair right across the table. Somehow, I just now observed how fashionable he was. I didn't know why these kinds of things turn me on out of nowhere now, but it's super-hot when boys – or men have a good fashion sense.

I checked him out from head to toe. Well, he never fails to impress. He wore an olive-green cashmere sweatshirt, which was a little loose on the neck, showcasing his perfect collarbones, and black jeans with white Jordan sneakers. Damn those hormones, which did not show any mercy on me at all.

I wasn't any less. I paired myself with a two-piece outfit: a white shirt and beige office pants. The classy look.

He tossed a fancy envelope on the table. "Open it," he told me with a poker face.

I opened it.I

saw a wedding invitation card in it. "What's this?" I asked.

"Can't you see, it's a wedding invitation to which you said, 'Yes' to go to," he replied. "Go on, check it out."

"Yeah, about that," I thought of not going as it was a family function. None of my parents said no or anything, but I thought it was someone else's wedding, and I didn't know the bride or groom, so really, it was not my place to be.

"No, no, no, no-" he interrupted, before I spoke the words that were tending to come out of my mouth. "You can't cancel on me, Alpha. If you do, swear to God I will murder you."

Listening to his threats made me actually question him, "Why do you want me to go to this wedding so bad with you?"

"Becauuuuuse-" I looked at him, awaiting his lips to complete the sentence. "Because I told them you were my girlfriend," he blurted out, and the bubble gum from which I was making small balloons popped.

"What the actual hell!" My voice rose, and so did my body. I pushed the chair back to leave when he grabbed my hand and told me to listen to the entire thing.

I sat down again.

"Listen, I had to tell them. They were planning on setting me up with their family friend's daughter. I already said no to going home, and if I would have said no to their choice of girl, surely, I would have been disowned," he further explained. "That's why I told them I already have a girl in my life."

"Did you show them my photo?"

"No. Why?"

"Okay. I have an idea," I said and took the seat back. "I'll find you a girl who will act as your date at the wedding. This way, we both win."

"Not happening, babe."

"Why?"

"I don't wanna take any girl to meet my family. What if she's crazy or what? My parents will think I am one." I gotta admit that Hades had a point. You can't just show up with anybody to meet your parents, "I can't take the risk."

"I promise to find you a sane girl," I sounded convincing.

"Still not happening."

"Okay, okay." I proposed another idea, "How about this: just go on one date with the girl, and I will find you. If you feel like she is good enough to go, take her. Otherwise, I'll go."

He nodded. And that's all the gratification I was looking for.

Chapter 7
Hades

It's 6:30 in the evening. I was standing in front of the mirror, trying not to admire myself more, but I couldn't help it. I looked too good. I only got dressed because I had to go on a date, which I was going to reject.

I only said yes because I couldn't resist her emerald eyes trying to convince me. I knew her tricks by now. She was too obvious with her schemes.

Heather told me to reach the restaurant 'The Waverly' at seven in the evening. She set me up on a blind date and paid for it in advance. It was kinda cool that a girl pays for the date, except she was not the one going.

I looked at the time, and I was already late from being frustrated over this thing.

I reached the restaurant fifteen minutes later. No wonder Heather's choice of place was so cool. Like I had been living here for so many years and still hadn't explored this place.

Two floors and a massive chandelier. Warm lights and ancient paintings on the ceilings. Elegant people were all around, and waiters were all in uniform. I now know why she wanted me to suit up.

I took my phone out of my pocket and saw the photo of the girl Heather had sent me, but I still couldn't pick her up from all this crowd. Heather mentioned that her name was Hayley. As I saw the photo, I discovered that Hayley doesn't possess the same sharp facial features as Heather.

I called for a waiter passing by and asked him for the reservation under the name of Heather. He led me upstairs and took me to the table on the balcony.

I looked over the table, and the date she picked out for me was already there, so I was obviously late. Definitely, I was screwed. Heather was gonna rail me up hard for being late.

I walked over to the table, and the date finally saw me. She stood up, and I pulled out my hand for a handshake.

"I guess I am the first woman who waited for her date for half an hour. Hi, I am Hayley Howey," she said with a soft voice.

"I am Hades Ages Hawthorne and really sorry for being late," I replied. "In my defence, the traffic was bad."

I gestured for her to sit while I did so myself. "Well, you know it's worth it. You are quite handsome."

"Thanks for the compliment." I was a little nervous here. I really thought I was not going to enjoy, but I saw her big brown eyes and tried my best to hate it. But too late. "So, how do you know Heather?"

She kept on telling me about how she and Heather had become friends, and I kept on listening to the words she spoke. I was hightened by her amazing humor than her face but still somewhere In my mind Heather was present.

She wasn't present on this date, yet every word that Hayley was speaking indicating her was more better than any of her previous story but still at the end of the date, only one thought wandered in my mind. HAYLEY WAS FREAKING COOL. Maybe as much as Heather.

Chapter 8

Heather

I looked at the clock hanging in my room, and it was already ten at night. I was pretty sure that the date must be over by now, or maybe something actually worked out between the two.

In about fifteen minutes, I changed into jammies, washed my face, and did all my skincare routine. I checked my phone only to see if Hades had called me, but he hadn't.

Why the hell am I waiting?

I walked over to my bag, settled it over the table, and took out the invitation. I didn't know if I even wanted to join. I couldn't help but let the thought sink in.

I opened the envelope again to check out the invitation. I grabbed what looked like glass.

It was phenomenal.

The glass edges were shaped perfectly, so it could not cut anything or hurt. The upper one-third of the glass was patterned with acrylic gold blossom leaves.

I looked at the rest and everything written down with date, time, and venue in the same font and size. All of it was in centre alignment except the name of the bride and groom.

Cicilia Hawthorne & Aristos Christonopuolos.

It was written in a big font in the middle of the glass invitation, in the same gold acrylic but with a different italic font.

I wondered if this was how all the invitations looked and what the wedding would be like. It was so pretty. I really wanted to join now, but it was not my place to decide now. It was up to Hades.

But it's okay, almost.

I placed the invitation back into the envelope and rested it inside my bedside drawer. I took out the diary from the same drawer and flipped to the pages from where I had to read again.

I fixed myself on the bed and started reading. The entry was directly on the 14th of May.

15th May 2020,
Saturday.

Hades entered Advance Mathematics the day before yesterday and wrote down notes for Heather, even though he only asked one favour in return: that she should come and watch his basketball game today.

It was a shock to his Alpha and me, both, that he never gave up.

When we showed up at his game, he acted normal, but he was surprised because he thought Heather would not. Joshua told me after the game how nervous he was.

*Our school won the game, hands down. It was only possible because of him, obviously. After the game, everyone wanted to click pictures with him, unlike us. We saw half of the girls crowd out of the boys' locker room, and a few of them were even taking selfies with teammates, as was Hades. Nevertheless, Hades was different from others. He was showing the backside of his jersey to everyone, indicating the number **09.** Last time, his jersey number was definitely not 09, but when Heather asked about it, he hesitated and spoke the truth later that it was her birthday date. She even asked about how he knew about it, and his exact words were, "You can't hide from me, Alpha."*

In my defence, I wasn't trying to betray my best friend, but I didn't want another guy to take my spot. So, I did tell him about her birthday so a love interest could take place.

I read this page and remember the good times, as well as found the rat who spilled my birthday. Weird thing was, he still wears the same number. Wonder why he never changed it when he had the chance. I flipped over to the next page and continued reading. I barely read the date when my phone started ringing.

It was Hades.

I was so happy he finally called. I picked up the phone.

"Hey! How was the date?" I asked as soon as I picked up.

"Open the door," he said.

"Are you outside my apartment?" I asked.

"Just open it," with a lower voice, he answered. He didn't even put any effort to make it cool, yet it seemed one.

I slipped out of my bed, jumped into my slippers without hanging up, and went across the living room to open the gate.

Opened the gate.

Okay, I saw Hades standing in front of me. Totally wasted from what I look at. He was looking down. One hand helping him lean against the door frame, and the other swinging by his thigh.

Looking at him, I could totally make out two things: either the date went terrible or - no, JUST TERRIBLE. I wondered what he did, even though he dressed awesome.

I mean, I checked him out up and down, and it made my temples sharp. He took my soul away, even though he didn't seek to. He listened to my advice about dressing awesomely on this date.

He finally lifted his head up and hugged me. My temples touched his chest while my head hung down from my shoulder.

"You sure have a nice arse," he muttered.

"Was this an indication of a booty call?" *Even if it's not, let's make it one.* I wanted to say this, but I had to get myself out of that imagination as soon as possible. It was wrong of me to do so.

"Nooo," he spread that word too long for me to realise that I actually had to ask about the date.

"How was Hayley?" I asked him while dragging him from the door to my couch. I pushed the door back with my foot and settled him on the couch.

"She was smart, beautiful, and everything a person could possibly look for in a woman, but you are still going to the wedding with me," he said in a drunken, husky voice.

"Why?" It was an obvious question. If he found everything that a guy wants in his girl, then why is he stuck taking me to the wedding?

"Because she ain't you, babe."

His words flushed over my face and got me all red. "You don't give up, do you?" I asked with a small grin.

"I can never give up on you, Alpha. Set that straight into your head. If you don't, I might have to make you scream to do so, and that doesn't involve any illegal activity." He notched his eyebrows at me. "Believe me."

I giggled.

"Oh, you think that's funny. You don't believe I can make you scream my name."

"No, I don't."

"How do you know? You've never even had sex."

"Comes from the person who himself hasn't lost his virginity. And, as a matter of fact, about my confidence, I read books, sweetheart. Fictional men get me on."

He pointed out a finger in the air to clarify, "I would have done it long ago. Even today, but I didn't. I wanted you to be my first and last."

I wish I knew he was serious or not. Every word he spoke seemed serious on various aspects; otherwise, I would not have got any jitters in my body. My heart started racing at those words, and I saw his chest rise and fall too.

"Planning on crashing here?" I did my best to avoid the tension.

He nodded.

I couldn't let him crash on the couch since it's super uncomfortable. First of all, he was too big to be fitted in a couch like that, plus it was cold out here. I was more worried how unsatisfying it was going to be for him to sleep in that outfit.

Just as I wrapped his arm around my shoulder, he soon flooded me with his body weight. He was heavier than he seems to be.

I helped him to walk over to the guest room, and opened the door, and threw him on the bed. I checked every cupboard possible after that to find men's clothing that was actually fit for him.

I guess I heard the door open, so I rushed into the living room. It was unlocked, but the knob was slowly getting twisted, trying not to make a sound. I knew it was Delilah.

I crossed my arms over to watch her attempt. Finally, I opened the door.

"AHHAHHA. You scared me, bitch," she rested a hand on her chest, trying to recover from the trauma I just gave her. "I thought you slept."

I did not bother to answer anything; I planned on giving her another trauma right now. "Do you happen to have any men's clothing?"

"I might have," she said. She didn't notice anything else and brought a few men's t-shirts and sweatpants back to me from her room. "Whom do you need it for?" she asked.

"Hades. He is crashing here tonight." Her mouth flew open when I took one t-shirt and sweatpants from her collection. "Thanks, by the way."

I went to the guest room and saw him lying in the same place I left him. He had not even turned. I finally woke him up by tapping him continuously and told him that a few clothes were on his side. If he wishes to change, he could move his ass up for it.

As I turned to leave, a sudden pull on my arm yanked me next to him. Damn, he was strong too. I saw him sit up straight now.

"You never answered," he said.

"About what?"

"Do you want to be my first and last?" I saw him looking at me very seriously, with no intention to let go of my hand, with no intention to hear about anything else but the answer.

Yeah, Not only do I want to be your first and last, but I want to be the only one. And everything you ever owned. I want you to stop using your mouth to flirt and kiss me hard instead. I want you to hold me and never let me go. I just want to be yours.

I snapped out of the vision. Staring into his eager eyes, waiting to know my answer. So, I leaned in and touched his lips with mine. "Guess it's late. You should change and sleep."

I wanted to kiss him more, devour him more, let every taste of his sink into mine. But I was his best friend. If something goes downhill, I would not only see him as a boyfriend but also as my friend. I couldn't afford that.

I entered my room, and my eyes became watery at that small kiss as I stood behind the door. Even if it was a peck, for me, it would be my first kiss. I walked back towards my bed and slipped myself into the sheets.

Chapter 9

Hades

I woke with the smell of pancakes and coffee. None of my staff makes breakfast when I strictly restrict it due to my basketball practice in the morning.

It was clear-cut that I needed no food before my practice. It was better to work on an empty stomach, but the smell was dragging me to the gates of gluttony.

After my practice, I like, to take a shower followed by my meal. Wondering what changed. I opened my eyes and was welcomed with the most plain ceiling in the world. No colours. Just white with a ceiling fan.

I sat up straight and looked around, and bits and pieces kept coming back to my head. Date. Alcohol. Heather's apartment. Clothes. Kiss. OH MY GOD, THAT KISS.

I checked every piece of clothing that I was wearing. Not fashionable. At all. Where did I put my outfit I wore yesterday? At least, kind of glad that Heather knew I needed comfortable wear to exchange my outfit with.

No wonder how good the room smelled, with her scent of strawberries and vanilla, but the clothing, it was still plain as shit. I climbed out of the bed, opened the door, and saw Heather in black shorts and an oversized white t-shirt. It was bliss to my eyes every single time.

She noticed me. "Rise and shine, big boy," she said.

"Well, good morning," I rubbed my eye while she tossed a plate in front of me and set the pancake in it a minute later. She held out the coffee jug and a cup.

"Coffee?"

"Yeah, sure," I took the cup from her hand when she poured another cup of pancake batter into the pan. "You don't drink coffee?"

"Have you seen me drink one in the last two years?" I shook my head for obvious reasons. It totally slipped my mind that Heather was a cranberry juice addict. "You got your answer, big boy," I was surprised, but it's true.

"Like you have never tasted coffee?" Since I have known her, she never drank a coffee in front of me.

"Never say never. I mean, I don't like it, but Delilah does, so I make it for her every day," she flipped the pancake and pressed it for more crisp.

"Oh." I took a long pause and then noticed Delilah, was nowhere to be found. "Where is she anyway? It's SUNDAY."

"She went to mom's."

"You didn't?"

"Someone had to take care of you, big boy." I love that nickname that she keeps referring to me with those pouty lips. I was embarrassed a bit that she had to stay home just for me, so I kept my focus on the delicious pancakes. "So, are you taking Hayley to the wedding?" she asked.

"No. Like I said yesterday, she must be everything a guy wanted, but I ain't like other guys. I want you. And I meant every word." I saw her placing the pancake on the plate and pouring some maple syrup on top.

She placed both of her hands on the kitchen counter and put her whole body weight on it. "You sure about it, Hades?" she hesitated.

"Three Thousand Percent," I replied while cutting the pancake.

She just gave me a smile. The lower dimple got me. *Why doesn't she smile often?* Everything about her smile was just so PERFECT.

I turned my attention back to the food rather than her smile, but I knew one day that this smile would haunt my dreams, my imagination, and most of all, my gentleness.

Chapter 10
Heather

"When's the wedding." Delilah literally yelled and threw every dress I own on the bed. Or at me for not telling her sooner.

"It's a JUNE WEDDING," I replied softly, "On the first."

"Ohh, that's early. It's the seventeenth already." I nodded because I knew that this yelling wasn't stopped just because she was shocked and used her silky voice to mock me.

The sad part of it was being, I had no idea if I had anything good to wear for the first time I was meeting his family. I knew he was extremely rich and I was not someone they knew. I had to make a good first impression.

"Not to forget, he actually told them I am his girlfriend," I said.

"It's going to be weird." I seriously searched my wardrobe over and over to find a few dresses but ended up failing every time until Delilah told me to shop right that moment.

Even if I had, say no, I would have ended up going there anyway. Might as well go with my best friend. At least she can do is help.

It took us three hours to buy two dresses, and that too without other stuff. We were walking out of the complex. "You told me the wedding is for three days," I heard Delilah say.

"Yeah."

"But you bought only two dresses when you should have at least six," she pointed out.

"They didn't have anything to match my taste."

"Babe, you gotta look hot," she said, and I eyed her for saying such a comment to my face. What did she mean when she used a phrase like that?

"I was born with my hotness," I said, flipping my hair to let her know that she might be talking to the next Aishwarya Rai. She was a Bollywood actress with the same eye shade as mine.

"I won't deny that!" a familiar voice came from the back. I turned around and spotted Hades in a white hoodie and black jeans.

"What are you doing here?" I asked him while also noticing Delilah smirking and moving her eyes back and forth between him and me.

"I came here to pick you up," he replied to my curiosity.

"Why?"

"It's game night, and you are coming with me," he grasped shopping bags from my hand while using his other hand to find a spot on my wrist. I held Delilah's hand and pulled her with me. "What are you doing?" he asked as I dragged Delilah along.

"If I am going, then she is coming too. Period," I told him, while my pupils expanded with a serious tone.

"Okay," he nodded.

It's been two hours, and my apartment was filled with basketball players. People were actually checking my room out. *Super humiliating.* And Hades telling them to stop it as it was his girl's room.

Seriously, now, I was HIS girl for the basketball team.

The game started a long time ago, and Delilah and Joshua both bailed on me since they didn't want to watch the game. Hades was not letting me get out of sight.

I got the centre seat on the couch while one of his teammates was sitting right above my head. On the headrest of the couch on my right. These guys were so 'eww.' How come Hades was so sophisticated and seated himself next to me?

All eyes were on the television. Few from the kitchen, and few were from every spot of my living room, covering while mine were attached to my phone. Currently scrolling on my bookstagram.

On the side, I was window shopping as well, and I went to every site I could to find myself a dress for the wedding. Oh, my cell slipped from my hands into Hades. I gave him a death stare. "Watch the game, Alpha," he commanded. "The last five minutes are left, and you have been on your phone for the whole game."

"I know, but it's boring," I wheeled.

"Just watch. It's not going to be after this last shot." He shot me a glance before slipping my phone into his pocket. I reached out my hand to grab it, but his other hand grabbed mine again. I kept on trying to release myself from his capture, but he was more powerful.

Still, I was trying to take it, but he was pushing it away as his hands were grabbing me closer, and I found myself fixed to his lap. Rolling his arm around my neck my phone fell. Using my other hand to grab it, he slapped my hand away.

I made a face and laid myself onto him, carefree, until I felt a little discomfort on my spine. I reached my hand up to my back and found the remote of the television.

Revenge time. I was going to make it dirty. A smirk showed up on my face, thinking of the perfect payback.

I grabbed the remote in my hand without anyone noticing. Too busy for all the losers in my apartment.

I waited up until the last moment and switched it off as soon as the ball was thrown for a three-pointer.

Everyone stood up with squeaky voices, like they had just seen a murder. My head slammed on the ground. "Oww." I held my head where I was going to get a bump, and every loser was looking for the remote to turn the screen back on as soon as possible.

I stood up with my right hand up, holding the remote from the edge and the other on my head, "Looking for this, bitches."

Everyone had their eyes on me, and Hades looked at me like he was going to chop me off and love every inch of it. He ran to my bedroom, and I followed and opened every drawer. I was curious for a moment about what he was planning to do.

"Found it." He recovered one of my childhood files, and I still couldn't hold onto his intentions at the present. The file he had had nothing except my report cards and certificates.

"What are you even going to do with it?" I asked, narrowing my eyes.

"Wait and watch." It sounded like a threat. No doubt.

He searched through the file, flipping over pages and finally took the paper out of the folder. I closely looked at it and figured out that it was my fucking birth certificate, "Put it back, Hades."

"You want to play dirty, I'll play dirty," he mocked me. My mouth opened to plead, and by that time, he had ripped my birth certificate into two. My mouth stayed open for a few seconds until his finger came in contact with my chin and pressed my lips together.

"What the heck did you just do?" I shouted at him.

He put a finger on my lips and said, "Shut up. You don't exist anymore."

"I mean," trying to complete my words, he ignored me and walked back into the living room. Everyone's gone and left the mess. Let alone the part that my birth certificate just ripped got into two pieces.

I turned back and saw the door closed right after Hades stepped out of the apartment.

Chapter 11

Hades

It had been four days since Heather got angry with me for ripping off her birth certificate. Nothing more than a dry text I was receiving from her.

I wanted to call her, talk to her, and listen to her voice while lying on my bed, but I remembered how frustrated she was with this whole wedding thing and her dresses. I have not yet told her that she should be careful around my family.

My family was lovable, but they could over dial their craziness. Plus, it was my first time bringing a girl home. For all these years I had been home and apart, I'd never mentioned a girl.

I have had a long-distance relationship once, and only Cicilia knew about her. Thanks to that one, I met Heather. It didn't last more than two months, but after her, if ever I talked to Cicilia about a girl, it was Heather.

I knew internally how much it would mean to Cicilia if she joined the wedding. I had been talking about her non-stop to my sister for two years straight. No wonder she was so curious to see who got me wrapped around her fingers.

My phone buzzed. I looked at my screen and slid down the notification instantly to check if it was from Heather, but it was from Hayley.

I liked Hayley. Her presence gave out positive vibes and made me think less about Heather. None of my activities or my friends could do that. She is a cool person, but I don't think I was the one for her.

Hayley: Hey, how are you doing?

Me: Hiii. Good.

Me: What about you?

Hayley: same.

Hayley: I was wondering if you would like to hang out if you are free this Saturday.

Me: I am actually going to my sister's wedding.

Me: We can hang out when I get back.

Hayley: Yeah, sure.

I kept my phone aside and shut my eyes to take a small nap before my evening practice for basketball. I wondered if Heather was going to be in the library if she was not busy packing.

Our flight is on the twenty-ninth, and I heard Delilah was also going to Greece soon. Guess my Alpha was busy with all the goodbyes and stuff.

I let every thought of her sink into my head when I drowned in sleep.

Oh, shoot! I was late when I saw the clock at three. Packing everything in a hurry, I kept each of my supplies for practice. And ran off to the court.

It took me a little time to reach the court, but still I was late. I saw around, but the coach wasn't there. I saw Liam, who is currently teaching a girl to shoot the ball into the basket.

Liam is one of my closest friends, and it was a blessing that he was in the basketball team. Our families are somehow connected, and I spent most of my time with him when I was not with Heather.

He wasn't available on the game night as he was trying to score, of course. If the coach had seen him with a girl on the court, especially during practice, he would surely be getting all of us a punishment.

I walked over to him, and the question I asked was not about the girl, "Where is the coach?"

"He said that he will not be available for two days," he replied.

"Then there should be no practice. Why did he call us?"

"He said to practice regularly, though I am using this time for my girl." I see the girl next to him looking with wide eyes, like she is falling in love, and I wanted to tell her about the fact he doesn't have much discipline and sleeps over with chicks half the time and never calls them back.

Bro code 01: Bros before hoes, so I just fist-bumped and went to the locker room to change for my practice.

By the time I walked out of the locker room and made my pace towards the court, I stopped as I saw Liam teaching basketball to another girl. I looked closely to recognise it because the face cut was somehow similar to someone.

It was HEATHER. That, too, is in our school jersey with a high ponytail.

What the actual fuck! In that jersey, why was she here and why Liam was fucking touching her hand and teaching her to play when it was supposed to be my job.

I stride towards them, and they were still looking at each other, laughing at each other. I was filled with rage. Didn't he know that she was Heather?

"Hello there," I said, seeking both of their attention.

"Oh, hi, Hades," she waved.

"What are you doing here?"

"Apparently, I am learning basketball," she gestured towards him, "and he offered to help."

"Do you know him?" Liam asked.

"Of course, she does. She is Heather." His mouth flung open, and he backed instantly away when I said that. He handed over the ball to me, and I encircled Heather's wrist with my fingers to take her to another court.

She frees her hand from mine. "I am still angry with you for ripping my birth certificate into pieces." Before listening to any more words, I picked her up and asked her if she really came to learn basketball or to see me, but she replied nothing.

"See, if you want to be coached, I am here for you, Alpha, but I am not letting another man touch you," I said.

"Put me down first!" she said calmly, and I respected her decision, so I placed her down. She looked into my eyes with her narrowed one, "Youuuuuu."

"I am an asshole," I said. "I agree." To this unexpected reply, her face chilled down. "I really apologise for ripping your birth certificate. Don't just suffocate my living by not talking to me. I need you. More than that, I want you."

She sighed, "It's harder to pretend to hate you when I see your face."

"I know my face is dashing."

She played a handful of punches to my arms, "Back up, big boy, on that statement and taught me how to shoot."

"Well, you don't tyre your pretty legs and watch my practice match." Since I was the captain, I was allowed to make the practice match flexible whenever I felt like it. It was one of those perks. I gathered every member of the practice court, and the match began.

The teams divided this time weren't something I supported, but I was too angry with Liam to pick him for my team. So, for obvious reasons, he was proving his worth in every way possible, winning against me and making me regret.

Though I am aware that he was unknown to Heather, was she out of her mind to choose him over me in this court? She was cheering for his team. Traitor.

All I needed right now was to push two points more until my team won. No matter how good Liam was, he was not better than me.

I passed my two opponents and aimed to shoot directly when the ball slipped through the net for another score point, adding to my side of the board. Everyone shouted, and none of them considered the other team a loser since we were all from one school.

I pulled up my jersey from the edge and wiped my face until Heather stood in front of me with her eyes fixed on my abs. I called out, "Heather," and snapped two fingers in front of her face until she regained consciousness. "Treat, isn't it?"

"I have seen better," she replied.

"Tell that to the drool on your face," I teased until another playful hand punch hit me in the arms, and I laughed it off like a silly simp. "Let me take a shower, then I'll drop you home."

"Yeah, please do. I have a lot on my plate to clean."

"Like?" I asked.

"Packing my luggage to go," she said.

I gave a small smile and countered, "I'd rather pack you in my luggage." She laughed and gave me a slight push so that I could go and change, "Be right back."

She nodded with her pressed smile.

Chapter 12

Heather

We had reached the airport two hours earlier, and the fact that Hade's driver was doing everything. He had a beautiful name, Ashton, and he did everything on cue, but Hades was an asshole to him.

I had never seen Hades behaving rudely to anyone. I mean, he was always so fun-loving, but he had been awfully weird in front of Ashton as if he didn't even care if he existed or not.

Ashton did everything, and I was told at the very beginning that the flight was booked by his sister, so it was first-class. There was approximately one hour to kill before the departure, and Ashton had already taken care of everything else.

Hades led me to a private waiting sector, and it was looking expensive from the outside. A bar on one side and incredible interior. For sure, he was on his private jet, rich.

I was used to travelling in first-class because my dad preferred it, but I disagreed when I could go for the economy. Class wasn't specified through that, but it was from your heart, and Hades agreed with that thought all along.

I saw Hades legs up on the table, drinking beer and offering me to join him to watch the cartoons. He was such a kid from his heart.

After half an hour, a girl came and instructed us to take our seats. I placed my bags, as did Hades. I was lucky enough to pack my books for this flight. I unzipped my handbag and took out *Defy Me* by Tahereh Mafi to read.

I loved her books, and nevertheless, I have read all her books and am completing this series. I have heard so much about Aaron Warner on bookstagram that I actually ended up buying it.

I didn't bring Delilah's diary. If Hades knew about them, he would create a big scene out of it. I flipped through the pages I had to read and started my journey with it.

A few minutes later, I saw Hades watching me and the book cover. He held the book from the corner and repeated the title.

He took it from my hand, and in a second, I snatched it away and started brushing it with my fingers. "Are you seriously cleaning this because I touched it?"

"Of course, I don't want your dirty hands to ruin Aaron Warner," I replied to him. Actually, I spoke the truth.

"Who is Aaron Warner?" he asked.

"Aaron is my love," I told him some things that he should know before even considering liking me. "Fictional men were always going to be above you."

"What about me?" Hopelessness could be found right in his eyes.

I touched his cheeks with my fingers and said, "Oh babe, you are nothing compared to Aaron. Believe me, if you read this series, you will fall in love with him just like I did." I was trying to make him read this series so he could at least get the idea that I like these kinds of boys. Or men.

"Sadly, I am not gay," he answered back while removing my fingers from his face.

I slipped my one finger to the page. I was reading, "You can always have exceptions, hon," I say to his comment. It was unbelievable for him that I could be in love with fictional men too.

Well, it was defined. Aaron Warner is too hot and madly in love with his girl. He was the kind of person who would shoot himself rather than see his girl get a small scratch on her little finger. He would burn down the world for her if he needed to. That kind of person I need. I want.

By the time I finished dreaming about Aaron in every possible way because he was FICTIONAL and focused on my reality, who was on my side, he was sleeping. My lips curved into a small smile, and I took my eyes off of him and adjusted my eyes back to the book.

I had been reading approximately five to seven chapters when Hades' head dropped onto my shoulder. I placed the bookmark on the page where I left off reading and enjoyed every moment of his head on my shoulder while closing my eyes.

Chapter 13

Hades

It had been an hour since we departed from the airport. The flight was comfortable enough, and I learnt that Heather was in love with someone who didn't exist.

Now, we had been sitting in the car for the last half an hour, and she hadn't spoken a word to me. I had to drag Heather to this wedding; otherwise, my family would have fixed me up with every other girl in the room. Granted, she would surely show more interest in my work and words than my money when I knew for real that was the opposite.

At least Heather would save me from such small talk every now and then. "We have reached." The car made its way into the gate while I alerted Heather about Hawthornes. I could see her whispering, '*Damn.*'

I looked outside the window and watched as my eyes fell on the things where Cicilia and I used to play. Everything seemed so overwhelming; I wanted to be back here but not leave L.A. at the same time.

"If I knew this was the location, I would have said yes immediately," she muttered the words.

I got my senses on track again, and the car came to a stop. I stepped out of the car, watching my family waiting to welcome us. They were trying to set me up with someone; thus, it was necessary to lie about having a girlfriend.

I could have brought Hayley to this, but Heather was exactly the kind of person my sister, Cicilia, asked for. My sister requested her personally after hearing about her on a daily basis.

She knew my family would not let her off easy. In addition, she was smart enough to step out of the car in a way that she owned the trace where they were standing. I introduced her to everyone one by one.

Nothing has happened yet to mess it up. We walked upstairs to make ourselves more comfortable in the lobby before our room got ready. Cicilia joined us as soon as she finished attending to her other guest and walked over to us. "I knew… you can make up for it."

"I had to… I guess, Aren't we family!" The words spilt out of my mouth with a small laugh, like word vomit.

"I wasn't talking about you, asshole. I was talking about Heather. I still don't know how she's putting up with your sense of humour." She turned herself towards Heather and furthermore expressed, "I am so glad to see you, and thank you so much for joining the wedding on such short notice."

"It's okay! I wouldn't have missed it for the world," she said.

I looked around to take a glance. A manager was making his way over to us to hand out the keys. Since we were the organisers and the owners of the resort, we could customise our suits, but it would have been out of context if we lived in separate rooms.

Only Cicilia knew the reality of our arrangement, but my parents were unaware that Heather considered me nothing more than a best friend. I guess this trip would help me change her mind.

Shortly after Cicilia left, the manager handed our keys to Heather's hands. I told her, "I'll get you a different room, don't worry. For now, can you just play along?"

"I don't mind sharing a room with you. We might not have slept beside each other, but we can stay in the same room. Moreover, there's always a couch available, but I need the dressing room, so as long as you don't bicker about that, I am cool with it."

She was so casual about the whole situation. I saw Cicilia coming this way again. She did mention to me that she wanted to talk to Heather, but I thought it would be at the party tonight. "Can I borrow her for a second?"

"Yeah, sure." I looked at Heather. I knew she was nervous as she was looking into my eyes.

I helped the attendant pick out our luggage and take it up to the right room while she took Heather across the room and introduced her to our other family members.

I could see how much my mom was adoring her, except I couldn't help but notice that my father wasn't present in the audience. *Not that I care-* still, it would have been a nice gesture to attend the guest at his daughter's wedding.

I left them alone and walked upstairs with the bellboy to show him the suite. My room wasn't on this floor. I was pretty sure that my parents would have ceased the entrance of the fifth floor where our rooms were. The rooms where we were staying in were barely a guest room.

Soon after I saw Heather walking inside the door. She was exhausted from all the greetings. "You want something to drink or to eat," I asked, knowing that she would never say no to food, especially when it was free.

She nodded. "Cicilia asked me to be one of her bridesmaids. I told her that I would let her know by tonight, but I guess I am going to say no."

"Why?"

"Isn't this your family function... yeah? They do think I am your girlfriend. Nonetheless, it doesn't give me any right to ruin your family pictures," she said so firmly, though I could see a tinge of sadness in her eyes because I knew she wanted to do it.

"You should do it. It doesn't matter whether you are my girlfriend or not. If she asked, there must be a solid reason behind it, and that is, she really likes you. She never takes me in a picture if I ain't looking good, and she asks you to stand by her side at the wedding. It really means a lot to her, and, in my opinion, you should do it." I saw her pulling her head down as she closed her eyes for a second and gave a small grin. My hand was on the telephone to ask for room service, so in continuation, I dialled the kitchen.

"Are you ordering room service?" she interrupted. "Isn't this hotel expensive? Take me out and show me around. I love your city already. I want to capture moments here, not to sit in the hotel all day."

"Sure," I replied. Obviously, for a few reasons, I never corrected her that this wasn't a hotel. This was my house. Aside from this fact, this was my only chance to spend more time with her, so I kept the phone where it should be.

"Give me a minute so I can change and join you."

She was wearing this black coat dress, which was almost touching her knees, with a net off-shoulder design and full sleeves, demonstrating the elegance she possessed. *She looked perfect*, yet I couldn't deny her decision. Therefore, I nodded and left the room in case she needed privacy, telling her that I'd be waiting in the lobby.

After about fifteen minutes of waiting, I saw her walking down the flight of stairs in a short white dress with a red flower clip in her open hair, sliding on her left shoulder. She was smart enough to wear sandals with strings wrapping around from her ankles in a criss-cross way to her calves rather than heels.

Most of the women wear heels to flaunt their beauty. Hence, a lot of them drag themselves and are not able to enjoy the real beauty of Greece. My sister was one of them.

She wore an overcoat of floral net patterns. The end of the dress was around her thighs, showcasing her smooth skin down. She wore a black pendant with her name engraved on it, which was dropping down on her cleavage.

It took her less than fifteen minutes to change, unlike other girls, which was highly impressive and attractive. Her skin was glowing for this vacation after all the stress she was going through.

"Is this dress okay for the environment here?"

"It won't cause any problem, don't worry," I eased her down.

"Mr. Hawthorne, your car is waiting outside," The manager interrupted, leading us to the exit where the car I requested was waiting. The guards hurried and strode faster than us to open the doors of the vehicle. As we both stepped into the car, Ashton drove off.

We were walking in Santorini, with a different colour on every window we passed through. Her hand was tugged around my right arm as we walked down, finding a nice restaurant to eat in.

Couple Alert, guys around!

She said no to so many places, yet on our way over, I made this reservation in a very famous one, but she wanted to walk and explore the city as we found ourselves somewhere to dine in.

All I thought at that moment was, *"Isn't she hungry?" She hasn't had a bite since morning. How come she is able to enjoy all of this with an empty stomach?*

The sea was right beside us. She made her way towards the edge and sat on it while admiring the view. She didn't flinch for a few minutes there until I took my place next to her, and she looked into my eyes when I said, "You know, you are a lot like the sea."

"How?"

"It's so calm and peaceful until someone angers it, turning it into tornadoes. It gives a means on the Earth to thrive, like you influence me," her eyes sparkled while I completed.

Her deep thoughts really saw through me. I love spending every second of my life with her. I don't regret losing a table in the restaurant, so I could just walk around and show her what she might get herself into.

She should have never let me be this close to her when she knew about this possibility. Her eyes were still maintaining the contact while I was trying to close the distance.

I saw a man on the other side of the path walking over with a camera in his hands and disrupting us, "Do you belong to the family of Hawthorne's?"

"No! I am sorry, you must have got the wrong person." The answer slipped out of my mouth while Heather's eyes were experiencing shock. I don't even have security here. I almost forgot that this isn't L.A; *I am well-known here.*

"Yes, you are. YOU ARE THE HEIR." The man responded with a grin, which was obviously creepy. No matter how rude my response was, that man, with a height of approximately five feet eight inches, gathered around fifty people in a few seconds just by shouting at the top of his lungs.

I saw Heather laughing, but she didn't know how this ends in most cases. I had no idea what to do, so I grabbed her wrist and started running without even noticing where to go.

We hid at a few places here and there until we found a clear spot covered with houses on the sides. We were relentlessly catching ourselves when she burst into laughter, "What was that?"

"Just my fans, Alpha." Her laughter was so infectious that I joined her after a few seconds. We shared laughter. When we started strolling again, I heard her stomach groaning. "Can we eat something now?"

"No, I am not hungry."

I stopped by and protested my hand over hers. "But I am." I called Ashton to find us and bring over the car.

In another minute or two, Ashton brought the car over, and we walked upwards on the stairs where he parked it. I turned around to spot Heather, but I noticed her climbing the flight slowly.

It took me a while when I glanced towards her feet and saw blood puncturing through her toes, making it difficult for her to mark around, "When were you planning to tell me about you being hurt?"

Her gaze lifted upward, and her lips tightened when she muttered, "Never."

"Really, you think you can walk through? in this state when it hurts this much?" I was angry that she didn't tell me immediately, yet she nodded. "So, walk!" This was challenging to her as it was altering her ego.

She took a few steps before "Oww," and pulled back.

"I knew it." I was worried enough not to let her walk like this, so I made her sit on the stairs and gently took off her sandals. "Let me see." Her hair was stroking down, which was comforting as hell to my skin.

The cut was deep enough and happened due to me pulling her to run out of panic. "You can't go around like this. Nah, this aren't appening." I yanked her up with both of my hands and told her to hold on tight while I curled them around her neck.

She did what I told her to. I picked her up, resting my one arm on her back to give support to her spine and the other one clutching her knees together. She was as light as a feather, so I tugged her close to my torso.

I could just feel the warmth she was passing in my body. Even though I was extremely cold with my expression, it never bothered her because she knew, at the end of the day, *it will always be her I will rely on.*

"Thank you!" she cut in.

"Seriously, you are thanking me?"

"It must be hard to carry me around when I am heavy." Heather closed her eyes, her expression pained. Does she really believe that she could be this heavy to tire me around. Oh my lord, girls are so clueless about men.

"What the hell!" You barely count for my pre-workout." Her small grin made me take a glimpse of her like I never wanted to look at anything more precious than her. Her smallest smiles light up the cold war. I was fighting to live; that's how much she meant.

Even though we were best friends, she and I casually flirted so much that almost everyone knew we had a spark. But then again, she denied every hell of humour or, for God's sake, rumour.

I spotted Ashton at the end of the stairs, waiting with the door open, for us to be welcomed. I looked at her again, and she was drooling over the white pullover I was wearing. Her head was resting on my shoulders as she slipped into the comfort of my body.

I slid her slightly and steadily onto the seat of the car so that her sleep didn't get disturbed. I, myself, entered the car from the other door and again pulled her in so her head could be rested on my thigh for general ease.

I threaded my fingers through her hair and stroked it until I felt her sinking into it. Looking down at her sleeping so peacefully made me want to tug her close to me, even though I couldn't.

The air outside the window at the present was of dusk. I could smell her strawberry scent all the way up to my nostrils, which was pleasant enough to make me drown in it, yet I had to control myself to shelter our friendship.

We reached our place in half an hour, and she was still fast asleep. I hated it, but I had to wake her up so that we could join the family dinner at eight o'clock. It was already seven then, and she hadn't eaten a bite since morning. Plus, she got herself hurt; she needed time.

As soon as the car was parked in front of the gate, I tapped her cheek twice and called her out to wake her up to let her know, "Hey, we have reached."

She woke up with her drowsy eyes as she was rubbing them and planning to get out of the car soon. The chauffeur opened the door as soon as I stepped out of the car, so did she after a few seconds. "Today was tiring," she said.

"You still had a pretty good nap."

She raised her hands and arched her back in agreement with my statement. We entered the elevator to reach our floor and found the room with clothes lying around, hence a messed-up room. "I am so sorry, I forgot to clean up," her eyes apologetically elevated.

"It's okay. You go and change for the dinner while I take care of the mess."

"You sure??"

"Pretty sure I am."

Heather took out a maroon dress and placed it on the bed. Furthermore, she took out the toiletries and went into the bathroom. When I heard the shower running, that's when I called housekeeping to clean up the mess. *I had to impress her.*

While the housekeeping cleaned, I unzipped my luggage to take out one of my finest tuxedos. Luckily, there were two bathrooms in our room. It didn't take much time for me to change. I stepped out of the bathroom when I saw around a clean bedroom, and Heather was still in the shower.

"Ouch." I heard a voice echoing from the bathroom when I went across the room without even knowing about the situation. Nonetheless, I knocked on it, and she replied with a shouting voice, "It's okay, Hades. It's the injury that's hurting."

"Are you freaking kidding me, Alpha! I am coming in 30 seconds. Cover yourself if you haven't." My voice came out in a soft yet commanding manner.

A few seconds later, I entered the bathroom when she unlocked the door. She was sitting on the slab of the wash basin with cotton continuously tapping on her toe, which hurt her. The cotton was turning red as time passed.

I took her in my arms again and moved towards the bed, where I placed her beside her dress. "Can I?" I asked before touching her.

She nodded.

I slid my fingers to her toes where I applied the unused side of the cotton. From our luggage, I took out an ointment which was in the medical kit and applied it where she got hurt and bandaged it. "I will be waiting outside the room till the time you get dressed, in case you need anything or any sort of help. Just call out to me."

"Okay."

Within ten minutes of me walking out of the room, I heard the voice unlocking the door. I turned my back to peek at it when I spotted her in a maroon strap dress with a deep v-line showing off the shape of her curves in a perfect shape. The dress was long enough to cover one knee while the other was open with a slit. The strap of the dress, which was just as thin as the pencil lead, was sewed with pearls, showcasing her shoulders with the perfect A-line. *She looked amazing.* I could feel myself getting aroused by it, but I couldn't take my eyes off her because I just wanted to devour her in my sight forever.

"Wow - I mean, wow." My mouth flung open, my eyeballs popping out when she grinned on the side of my lips, where I could see the shiny lip gloss that I wanted to taste with my lips. "You look stunning."

She smiled.

She locked her hand on my arm before locking the door when I saw her foot worn by heels. *Why does she have to wear heels?*

We still went downstairs, and the usher guided us to our chairs for the rehearsal dinner. Before we took our seats, we greeted everyone, and I introduced her to almost every member of my house.

The bell for the dinner rang a few minutes after my parents sat down for dinner.

Chapter 14
Heather

Oblivious as I was after drinking two red wines at dinner, I couldn't stand upright. I was chit-chatting with a few of Cicilia's friends, but Cicilia herself was not there. I saw Hades on the other side of the room, who seemed like he was negotiating deals with the limited circle of his dad's friends.

"Hey! Are you free right now?" A slick voice carried from the back. I turned around to recognise the sound when I spotted Cicilia.

She was already a goddess, which brings heaven on Earth, and the dress she was wearing that night literally wanted me to kill myself. She was looking drop-dead gorgeous.

"Yes, sure." We strolled out of the dining room to get some fresh air. Walking on the aisle of the garden leading somewhere.

We talked about casual stuff until we reached in front of an ancient cathedral on the other compound of the hotel. We walked inside the cathedral when she touched my shoulder, "You know this is an ancient cathedral, built by our family's forefathers. It is said that once a promise is made in the oath of heaven, the bond will be protected by Aphrodite. My parents got married here, my grandparents too, and their grandparents too…. I am soon going. I am just getting cold feet about this whole commitment thing. Their marriage lasted, but it doesn't mean my marriage will. I love Aristos a lot, but love isn't the only thing needed to work in a relationship." She wiped off a tear from her cheek and went towards the candles that were already lit to make a wish.

I was looking around, and it was the most beautiful church I have ever been in. The Greek paintings on the ceilings were calling out only one thing - blessings. Cupids on the columns supporting the roof, and chandeliers lighting up the whole church like the sun.

I saw Cicilia in front of candles, and above her was the Greek Goddess Aphrodite, also known as the goddess of love. Well, it was a shock that Hades' name was inspired by the God of the underworld, while they could have named him anything. I didn't know much about Greek mythology, but I was curious to ask about it.

I followed her. A few seconds later, I shadowed what she did.

I closed my eyes to ask for something, but as soon as I did, I couldn't find anything to ask for when I already possessed everything I had, except him, I guess.

A tap on my shoulder from Cicilia disturbed me when she exposed a black box from her bag and insisted that I wear the sandals inside. I did what she asked. They were highly elegant and maroon in colour - *parallel to my dress* - comforting my sole with the cushions inside, draping a pearl string from one end to another, making a smooth brush against my skin with its coldness.

"So, what's your answer about being my bridesmaid?" she asked as soon as I stood up after wearing them… She, too, did the same to be on the same level as me while looking for an answer in my glare, in hope.

"I'll do it," I said.

She sighed and hugged me instantly when I felt this sisterly connection with her getting stronger.

"By the way, sandals are from Hades." With stress relieved from her face, she completed, "He saw you in pain with those heels when he requested me to give you these ones."

"Can I ask you one thing?"

"Yeah, sure," she said.

"Why is Hades' name on the name of the God of the underworld?"

She smiled and closed her eyes while looking down, and the smile grew bigger with a shake of the head. She placed a hand over mine, moved her gaze to Goddess Aphrodite, and said, "I don't know much, but my parents always told others that they want Hades to remain loyal to his one person like the God of the underworld did. Hades was loyal to Persephone. Unlike other Gods, he always loved her only and never used his power to overcome her. Similarly, they want our Hades to find a love he will be loyal to."

I nodded. The fact that Hades said things such as *I am his girl, she belongs to me*, and casual flirt. I thought it was all a game or a put-up Netflix drama, but what put him in a whole new light in my eyes?

My eyes were filled with happiness and love. I don't know, but I know for sure that he liked me, and maybe I liked him too.

Shortly after she finished, I saw the giant gate of the entrance being opened. I saw Hades walking in, but surprisingly, he was alone. "Here comes the devil. I should leave. Don't do anything stupid; God is watching." My eyes filled with tears when I saw her smile a little before she turned her back towards me with the intention of leaving.

I saw him walking towards me, looking handsome as hell. *My eyes were burning, as was my core from the hotness he was overloaded with.* I saw Cicilia passing by him, giving a wink, while he replied with a smirk.

"So, she told you about this place," he took a stand beside me, facing towards the candles.

"Yep, she did," I said. Nervousness was tripping over my words when I added, "Why did you ask Cicilia to bring me these sandals?"

" **Pretty shoes take us to pretty places**."

"Which pretty places are we talking about?" My tone sounded more teasing than it was in my head. I crossed my arms around my chest because I could feel my temples were getting rocky enough to slice a diamond at that point.

"ME!" *I loved the confidence he was showing.*

A small laugh came out of me until he made contact with my eyes without tearing them off for minutes, just staring right through my soul when he shouted words, "I am here to take an oath!" He took my hands and held them tightly in his palms, squeezing them gently - finalising his words, he echoed in the empty cathedral, "I, Hades Ages Hawthorne, make a promise to Heather Kades, in the presence of the goddess of love, Aphrodite, that my soul, is for her. I know she might trade me for a Subway Sandwich, but I never ever had a fake laugh with her, neither did she. I sure love my own company, but I would never leave her because she makes me happier than anybody else in this world because…. She - Is - My - Best Friend. She has been a shoulder to cry on for me in my ups and downs; I will do the same for her. If there is a possibility of another universe-"

He untangled my threaded fingers from his and cupped my cheeks with both. "I want you in every one of them to complete me because, without you, I am like a window that has never been closed. I don't need anyone else to make me believe in love because I have you to prove it."

He traced off every inch of tears that were falling down my cheeks with his thumb and a hand that was resting half on my it and half on my neck. Just being a few inches from his face, I really wanted to him, but I couldn't.

"I made you cry, huh!" he said. "That just proves how generous I am!"

"How come you can claim yourself generous from this?" I removed his hands from my face and grasped them in mine firmly.

"I didn't make it filthy. Otherwise, you would have been stripping for me right here, right now." That gawking eye, with a smirky smile, got me out with a grin. He grabbed my lying heels and pulled my hand into his palm instantly after I asked him about the time in order to leave.

We'd barely reached the porch after walking out of the church when I saw the blanket of stars covering us from above with the charmed moonlight.

Felt like I just saw an imaginary world of Van Gogh's art.

He ran to the midway of the path, gazing upwards to consume the beauty that was displayed. The freezing water, in the form of snow, was pouring down, "Wanna Dance?"

"Yeah, sure." I made my steps near to him with the same purpose as before until he poured out his hand in my direction. "You meant, like, right now!" I said while he held me in his arms, supporting my spine.

He was craving the touches he wanted to feel from me, which were unknown to him. I could sense it from his gentle placing of his hand above my hip. "Stupid, we have no music." It was the weather of Norway out here, yet I went on with his wish.

"Who said we don't have music?" That question got me into mild curiosity when my stare widened. I observed him closely when he yanked me towards him. I found myself fisting his shirt. His grip on my waist tightened, as did mine on him. "I Love You and Meee-Dancing in the Moonlight." He sang parallel to the song from my favourites, which I listened to on repeat; he must have learnt the words.

I wish I could take out the batteries of the clock that the universe holds, to stop the time for us, to be stuck here inside this moment, and enjoy this forever.

I want to tell him that *I might be in love with him* in every second we hold, but if the time has really taken a pause - seconds don't matter, I'll tell him that he was mine with each breath I inhale. I know he was on from me, but the time we were holding right now was infinite. When I perish from this place, he will restart the clock to begin the time.

He continued, "*Nothing in the world could make me feel the way you do…*" He might be the one singing those lines, but then again, I was the one having the sensations of them inside me. All the moments I had lived, yet I was pretty sure that it was going to be counted as one of my favourites.

As he was pulling me closer to him, I could smell the scent he was giving away. I wanted him to smell me and kiss me. My urge to kiss him grew stronger second by second, but it could just turn worse if he didn't return it.

I took all my chances and crashed my mouth against him. He returned it by sliding his tongue into my mouth. My eyes closed as we kissed, and thunders were crashing behind my mind. I felt zoned out when he sucked on my lower lip and, little by little, teased me with his tongue in between. Without even existing in the present, I felt my back touch the cold pillar that was on the side of the path with night lights on it. These lights were unnoticeable until my closed eyes felt some flashes upon them.

His hand released mine and went downward directly from my waist to my thighs. The feeling of them swirled around a bit until he skillfully reached the most sensitive part of my body.

Slowly, his hands were lifting up the dress, and the only thing that was separating his hand from my bare body was the cloth. But he never thought of it as a problem because I felt his fingers circling around the soft part, feeling like he was touching me in real.

His two fingers started rubbing the satin-laced cloth that was untying us, and my hands took the support of the pillar when his lips went to my ear, and he whispered, "Tell me. Is this what you have imagined, Alpha?"

The soundless moans kept on going, and his soft lips twirled between my cheekbone and my lips. The kiss broke into parts but never took a long break. His fingers never stopped either, until the night ended with me getting perfect pleasure.

Chapter 15

Hades

I was the groom's man, and Heather was the bridesmaid. We were going to walk down the aisle together, no matter what. It was my dream to do so with her.

My imagination was quite different than she was going to walk down the aisle when I took her hand into mine.

In an hour and a half, the ceremony was going to start, and I couldn't wait to see her anymore. I bet she looked phenomenal. She knew, at some point, I still loved her the way I did.

Hell no. I didn't know that at some point I would actually feel more for her than I have ever done for anyone. She came and messed up my life with the love she expressed all this time.

I was walking down the aisle with Heather's hand wrapped around my arm. I saw the end of it and spotted my brother-in-law who was waiting for my sister. Our God waiting for them, and the audience waiting to see this.

Heather and I separated at the end and took our places. Rings were in my pocket, and the tune of the background changed.

Everybody stood up, and I saw Cicilia walking down with my father. I turned my head towards Aristos, whose eyes were filled with water. I guess that's what real love is.

I saw Heather, and she was happy, but I did not see myself crying over her when she was looking like the moon that shines in the dark sky.

I loved her. I knew that much from inside, but something felt off.

The ceremony was indeed exquisite. The rings were exchanged, and the feelings were expressed in the form of vows. The couples were dancing, including my sister and brother-in-law, at the centre. The band was playing romantic music, and the lights were dimmed, except for the spotlight on the bride and groom.

Heather was standing next to me, and she looked as rare as pearls.

"Do you like me?" she asked me, completely off guard.

"No." my impulse reaction had no idea that my words would twist to this moment.

She sighed with a small smile. "I thought if you would have liked me, I would have convinced you to dance with me."

Relaxation washed over my mind. "Ask me anyway."

"Would you like to dance with me, Mr. Hades Ages Hawthorne?" Oh My. I could just feel an arrow of cupid just went through my heart. Those doe eyes looking forward with an innocence and all I could do was just manage to take a deep breath in and exhale.

"Sure." I poured out my hands, and her soft palm slid into it. Her hand was surprisingly cold, and I still wishedly that to hold on to for eternity. I draped my other hand around her and pulled her closely.

I could feel the beats of her heart against mine as she slowly put her fingers on my neck. People dance in the same way, with one hand in the hand of the partners while the other is on the shoulder or waist, but Heather dances differently. She did not put her hands on my shoulder, but she rested them on my neck.

I took her in the middle of the room, which slowly became empty. At that moment, I felt it was me and her and nobody else. She was the only one I had my eyes on, and no one could ever shine as bright as her. Her warmth felt like a winter sun, and her eyes felt like the ocean in which my presence of living lies.

At every moment, I feel the quote that Charles Bukowski once said: *Find what you love and let it kill you.*

Chapter 16

Hades

I was exhausted after re-joining L.A. from the wedding, and so was Heather. She had been sleeping since the previous day. I had dropped her home and then came back to mine.

At that time, I was out waiting for my date to arrive. I wasn't expecting to say yes but I had promised Hayley to hang out with her when I would be back from the wedding. I had not told Heather about it yet, and I was already feeling hell guilty. I was only here to let her know that there was a better man out there for her, and I love Heather. She was the only girl my eyes crave for, so if she plans for a future, then I won't be able to agree upon it.

Speaking of the girl, she was here in a short purple dress and pencil black heels, and her hair was done up. She looked incredible. "Sorry, I am late," she said.

"It's fine," I replied.

She dropped her purse on the patio table and took a seat in front of me. I decided on this restaurant, whereas she decided on the rest of the *get-together's* itinerary.

Last time, when I went authentic, I really wanted to hang out casually this time and gave her no idea of being interested. No drama whatsoever. The waiter came into our sight and handed out the menus to both of us. "What are you planning to have?" she asked.

"I have no freaking idea. What about you?"

The awkwardness between us was a bit obvious, and I guess I was the cause for it. It took us a lot of time to decide on the food that we both like, to consider for eating.

We both ordered our choices and as we ate our meal, I was curious to ask her, "What's the plan after this?"

"I wanted to check out this bookstore nearby, so I thought we could do it together."

"Sure," I told her.

After finishing our food, we walked to the bookstore rather than taking any vehicle. The store looked pretty huge from the outside and so old-fashioned, like I have probably seen in movies and stuff.

We walked inside and started exploring books of our own genre. I didn't know much about her, but seeing Hayley wandering around the mystery section made me sure that she likes thrillers and suspense books.

I was walking around in the store when I reached the romance novels section. My eyes fell on a book which captured my attention like none other. The book, of course, was SHATTER ME.

The whole date went incredibly, yet somehow, now that I have seen this book, I couldn't get Heather out of my head. And the fact that I hadn't told her I was here on this date.

I picked up the book and asked the helper there to give me every one of its parts. I wanted to give it a read because Heather couldn't seem to take this fictional character *'Aaron'* out of her head, and I was going to make that happen and replace him with the real one. That's going to be me.

I slammed the six books and three novellas on the counter and asked the employee to bill it right now. Hayley came back with two books in her hands. She looked at my book, "Oh, I see, you like romantic ones."

"No, actually. Heather told me to read this series, so when I saw it, I thought of buying it."

The facial expression of Hayley changed from amusement to jealousy in seconds at the mention of Heather's name. She was the one who introduced us, so why does she seem jealous?

"Oh." Those were all the words she had said to me.

Soon after, I dropped her where she wanted me to go and headed to Heather's apartment, though telling her how much I felt for Heather slipped my mind.

I reached over to her house by four in the evening, hoping she would be awake by then.

I knocked at the door, expecting to see my girl. Instead, a boy greets me. What the actual fuck? Who was he?

He is approximately five feet and ten inches tall, with light skin coloured and hair as a fuck. Boy types. Eyes brown as Delilah and dressed neatly.

"Yes. How may I help you?" he said while blocking the view by standing in front of me, but his height was not big enough to do so.

"I am Hades, Heather and Delilah's friend. Who are you?" I introduced myself for the sake of human courtesy. He opened the door wide and invited me in.

"I am Chase Omen, their roommate," he explained, and a shock ran over me. I can't let a boy live with my two best friends. "Delilah," he shouted, "Hades is here."

The door opened wide, and Delilah came into view. She waved at me, and so did I. The awkwardness spread, and Chase excused himself to his room.

As soon as he locked the door of his room, I panicked and asked, "Does Heather know that a guy is also living here?"

"Not yet. She has been asleep," she said, standing up and walking towards the kitchen.

I followed her and said, "Dude, it is so not cool for a guy to live with two girls."

"He is gay." Oh my, relief took over, and my mouth flew open at the answer she told me.

"Are you sure?" Surety is the best policy here. Boys sometimes act gay to stay with girls.

"Yeah, he has a boyfriend. I met him, and he is also hot." She placed two glasses and a cranberry juice to offer.

"Anyway, when is she gonna wake up?" I asked, pointing to Heather's door.

"She was really exhausted from the trip, and before unpacking, she was not ready to sleep. Because of that, she slept around three in the morning." She took a sip of her juice and completed, "How come you are awake?"

"I went to a get-together."

"With whom?"

"Hayley," I replied.

She choked on her juice, and I didn't realise that it was such a big deal until now. "What!?" Her voice went on a larger scale, and her expressions were on a different one that I couldn't even get to explain.

"Heather made me meet this girl named Hayley, and she was good enough," I told Delilah everything about how I met her and how she asked me for a date, but I couldn't go because I was going to the wedding.

"Can I meet her?" That's all Delilah asked me "Sure," I nodded and finished my juice. The door to another room opened, and Heather walked into the kitchen without noticing me.

Rubbing her eyes, she took the cranberry juice and slid a cup onto the table for her to drink with half-opened eyes.

Even if she didn't notice me, seeing her like this was what I lived for.

When she finally drank the cranberry juice in a minute and slammed the cup on the counter, she finally noticed me, and her eyes widened with shock.

"What the fuck, Hades? What are you doing here?" she shouted, and another door opened. Chase came in to join the drama. She pointed at him with her finger, "And who the fuck are you?"

"He is our new roommate," Delilah introduced.

"Hi," he waved at Heather with awkwardness and finished, "I am Chase Omen."

Another day started for Heather, but shock and panic overwhelmed her, leaving her speechless. As I see it, her mouth was still open.

"Don't worry about me. I am gay, not even bi, and I have a boyfriend," he further added.

"Oh, okay." Another round of awkwardness goes around.

I pulled out my keys from my pockets. "I think," I said, "I should leave." I started walking towards the door, and Heather followed when I told her that I would call her tonight to fill her in with an update.

Chapter 17
Heather

I arrived home at nine that night. I was busy all evening getting to know more about our new roommate, Chase Omen. Apparently, he belongs to the French ethnicity. His face showed no mercy on girls, just like his choice of living.

My imagination kind of worked up like Hades' because when Delilah shared with me that Hades was worried that certain men would pull off these stunts to live with girls, I believed it. In fact, due to this thought, I checked thoroughly after he visited.

More of it, the way Chase had powers to charm people just by his elegance might be at the top of my list to achieve before this year comes to an end. It was funny that hanging around with him for just a few hours made me spill all my tea with Hades.

Every interaction I remembered from the start to the end. The most thrilling part was that I lived every moment while I elaborated every second of my *life* to him.

I changed in another few minutes and directly called Hades in my call logs.

He picked up in another few seconds before it could reach the second ring. It was like he was waiting for me to call.

"Hey, Alpha!" he called out.

"Hi," I replied. "Are you busy?" It was justified to ask this question when I just met his family and got to know more about him.

"NO."

"So, what did you want to share?"

"I met Hayley today," he informed, "I hung out with her. First at a café, then went to the bookstore."

He continuously went on and on, informing me everything about his so-called get-together, but how could I just tell him that this was indeed a date, whether he realised it or not?

Well, I wasn't jealous until he mentioned that she was upset that Hades had bought all the "Shatter Me" series based on my suggestion.

Why was she the one who was angry when I was taking it very calmly? He only bought some books on my advice.

This was beyond my understanding, yet I tried to explain to him, "If you liked her that much, just try to understand her feelings. If she doesn't like to talk about me, then I guess you should not mention me in front of her."

"For obvious reasons, she does have a cute personality, which I can't seem to get rid of," he said.

Jealousy intervenes, but support is important here, "then you should ask her out."

"What are you even saying?" he snapped.

The conversation continued, "It's not like we are in love with each other or something." *Obviously I love him*, but at this point, I just couldn't be out with my feelings when I know for sure that he was liking this girl.

"Oh, that's what you think!" he countered.

"I don't think that. I just stated the reality."

"Cool then," his voice rumbled. Without me being able to say any more words to defend myself, he hung up on me.

Hades

How could she ever state that we were nothing? Why does she think that? I thought I was very upfront about how my heart felt for her, but if she thinks so, then maybe she never thought of me as that guy who could ever be in love with such a beauty.

I missed her in every sleepless night and yet I received no answer as such. Heat rose on my face, so I had to leave the call before it got more embarrassing for me.

My pride screamed in moments to get out of the call and ask Hayley out on a real date, as my way of getting even with Heather.

Chapter 18

Heather

I stood in front of the mirror and realised that I looked perfect in those olive green gym shorts with an oversized white tee. To accessorise it better, I wore gold earrings that were gifted by my parents for Thanksgiving and a white hat. My hair was open, and I looked like a woman with perfect curves.

It's been two weeks since the talk between Hades and me took place, and he hung up the call in my face. We have been a bit distant since then, but he was genuinely sorry afterwards. Even with all the sorting out, he never mentioned the fact that he still had feelings for me, so I assume he does not have any.

Maybe he lost feelings after the kiss. It's quite common in men that the person they had been waiting for kisses them for the first time, their feelings just disappear. Well, who am I to comment on anything? All I know is that I had to leave with Delilah and Chase in the next five minutes to join the basketball match to which Hades invited me.

As I was watching myself in the mirror, the door opened, and Delilah peeped in. She was wearing the same outfit, except her colour palette was way different from mine. "Ready to go?" she said.

"Yeah. Let's go and kick some ass of other schools," I replied while taking one last look into the mirror and walking out of the room with her.

As we came out, I saw Chase dressed up elegantly, even for a basketball match. He said, "Let's move it," when he saw two of his most beautiful girls come into his view.

We walked out of the apartment, and I locked the door behind me, slipping the keys into Chase's hands.

We took the front seats half an hour ago before the game started. The game was on at that time with a score of thirty-nine to forty-two. The higher score was from our school team, of which Hades was the captain.

Well, I guess for Hades, this was more of a practice match, as he had played for states several times. Plus, I knew our team would win because Hades never missed any of his practices, even when it came to warming-up. He worked really hard that year, hitting the gym often as well.

I felt a phone on my side vibrating. In a moment or two, I saw Chase slipping the cell into his hand. I peeked to see who it was from. "Excuse me. I have to take this," he sought permission.

"Yeah, sure," I replied. As I said the words, he moved his ass out, the gathering moved towards the washroom. Hopefully.

As I checked out the game again, it was getting serious because another team had just scored, which credited them with two points, and the ball was still in their favour. I took a stand on my seat and shouted, "You can win this game, Hades. I know you have worked really hard," I stated what he needed to hear while the crowd went silent behind.

I caught his attention, and I was looking at him with the hope that he would win if he gave his best. Everyone's gaze was on me, and mine never stopped anywhere but him. And him only.

He smiled and reverted his attention back to the court. The voice in my head started appearing again. The worst mistake made by the opponents was dribbling the ball near Liam, where, without a second's waste, he punched it in his favour. The ball passed around the court as if it was barely touching the ground.

Until it finally reached Hades' hands. He stood on the big D and jumped. The crowd once again went silent because only ten seconds were left on the clock. Even without this, we would win, but the winning basket should be made by the captain; otherwise, Hades will be upset for at least a few months.

The ball swirled around the rings until it finally went through and touched the wooden floor. Everyone stood up and started cheering for him. His teammates ran towards him to hug him while I was standing where I was supposed to be and just smiled at him amongst the crowd.

He looked at me from the crowd and yelled, "That was for you, Alpha." Everyone looked back and forth to us while our eyes never departed from each other. The tension between us was obvious, and just by looking at him, I knew that he just wanted to see me in the locker room.

My eyes were fixed on him when the member of the opposing team, who had just lost, threw a ball right at his face, rendering him unconscious as he fell onto the wooden floor. Everyone gasped around him. Half of his teammates were picking him up, while the other half were ready for another match, just not with the ball.

I got down from my chair and told Delilah that I was going to check on Hades. Not wasting any time, I ran outside the court.

As I was striding fast in the corridor and finding the turn where another corridor begins to lead to the locker room, I saw Chase standing next to the water cooler. He was shouting at something and seemed quite upset.

I reached towards him instead of moving forward. I placed a hand on the back side of his shoulder, with my eyes worried. He hung up the call as I asked, "Everything's okay?"

"Yeah, everything is fine," he said.

"Are you?"

"Yes, I am," he said in the most fake voice he could have ever used.

I turned my eyes towards him and confirmed, "You sure?"

He sighed, "Maybe not. I don't know what should be done when I am stuck in a situation like this," he said.

"Want to share?" I asked.

He nodded.

We both moved towards the bench placed in front of the water cooler and seated ourselves. I placed my hand on him, and he began his saga. I was listening very carefully.

Hades

Heather and I were in the fields of sunflowers with the sun overhead. Enjoying the sun, she was running in the fields. I, however, was feeling a bit weird when I saw the sunflowers facing downwards instead of upwards. It was a feeling like something insane was going to happen.

The warm sun was giving out its heat, and I was standing there for only a few seconds when I noticed that Heather had vanished into thin air. I called out for her to check if she was sitting somewhere in the fields, but none appeared to be there.

I tried to walk, but suddenly, I felt like my legs weren't working. It was like paralysis below the waistline. I couldn't move. I looked back for a few minutes and called out for her until the changing weather caught my attention.

It started to turn from warm weather to cloudy weather. The clouds were closing up the sky with their darkness. I looked back at the fields and saw Heather in front of me.

Her eyes were filled with rage, and her hair turned into snakes like Medusa. It was as if something worse had taken place in my absence. Even with that outshining appearance, her soul screamed purity.

I shouted, "Heather."

"Heather," I called out as I saw a blurred version of Heather with my half-dimmed eyes.

"Hades! It's me," the voice was familiar but not of the one girl I was used to hearing. I closed my eyes for a brief moment and opened them again, where I spotted Hayley.

I started to wonder if I had brain damage. I was looking at Hayley, and yet I was trying to find the symbolism behind the dream I had just had.

Placing a hand on my head, which was paining, I planned to get up from the bench. I saw everyone around asking if I was okay, but concentrating on Hayley's expressions, I could very well make out that she wasn't.

"Everyone is requested to give us a moment alone. Me and Hayley," I said.

Everyone respected my decision and moved out of the locker room to give us some privacy. I mirrored the same way she was sitting and placed a hand on hers like she did before I came back to consciousness.

"Something happened? You seem a bit upset," I stated.

"I am worried about you," she replied.

"Nah, that's not it."

As she looked towards the floor, with a saddening tone, she continued to say, "Well, you called out for Heather instead of me."

"Then, it doesn't matter," I replied.

"It surely doesn't matter to you, but it does to me," she pulled her face up from the floor and stared right into my eyes with her brown ones. "It quite doesn't add up that whenever you feel low, you always call out for her. If she means a lot to you and vice versa, I would be happy in your happiness."

"Nah, babe. Nothing of that sort had ever happened between us," I lied. "We are just best friends."

In reality, we both knew that I was lying.

"You called out for her when I was here with you, so I guess that means more," she said.

"There is nothing you should be afraid of," I defended.

She nodded and took her eyes off me.

Chapter 19
Hades

Two months later...

Apparently, Heather just indirectly told me that Chase matters to her more than I do. That dude just broke up with his boyfriend, and she is giving him more attention than I ever got.

I mean, I understood that Chase was sensitive, and now that Delilah was also moving away. He was going to stick with her ALL DAY. *What the fuck!*

It was sincerely planned that day that Heather and I had to go shopping today, but her dumb new roommate just got stood up, so she was with him.

In the end, I ended up calling Hayley to spend some time with me. Anyways, I had a free holiday on my hands which got cancelled. Better than bingeing Netflix, I thought.

Hayley and I were in a phase where we were in a relationship. It was kind of going slow. We had been on dates - if we can call so - and I told Cicilia about her, but she doesn't support me with any other woman other than Heather.

Right now, waiting in the car for Hayley to just open the door and slide in with her smooth skin and tell me what she did today. Though it was not always as interesting as talks with Heather, but I loved it anyway.

"Sorry, I am late," she said from the opened window and opened the door of the car. She sat down on the passenger seat while her thighs grabbed my attention. Tan lines made her white dress blurry, and she looked pretty.

"It's okay," I said.

"I got you a present," she said, full of curiosity, and caught my attention, apart from her thighs. She took out a big velvet box from her handbag, big enough that it wasn't a proposal one.

"What is it?" I asked.

She flipped open the box, and a Rolex shone right into my eyes. "It's GMT Master II in yellow gold oyster steel." I was amazed. I mean, it was so beautiful, but my hand was covered.

"I love it," I said, but I couldn't express it because even though I wanted to take her watch into my hands, I was already wearing Heather's grandfather's watch.

She pulled out my wrist-

"Get out of her room, guys," I said to the people who were currently standing in my girl's room. She held her head when she saw that the game night was proposed to be at her house.

Even though I am the captain, they hardly listen to me because I am too nice, and Liam keeps them on track.

This time, as a captain, I said the same words with a firm voice, and everybody started making their way to the living room. Delilah didn't care if someone was actually going to her room, and she took off with Joshua.

As I was showing myself out from her room, I saw a diary on her bedside drawer, lying under the shade of the lamp.

The book was labelled 2020. I shouldn't. I kept reminding myself I shouldn't invade her privacy, so I opened the upper drawer and kept it.

Right on the side of the diary, I saw an old watch. I remember the day of the grandfather's funeral when she slipped his watch into her hands so she could cherish it as his memory of him. And from what I saw, it was the same watch.

"I can't believe I am going to do this," I said into the air.

I grabbed the watch and slipped it into my pocket. I closed the lights, left the room, and walked back to the living room.

Since then, I have been wearing her grandfather's watch. It was dear to her, and I kept it for myself to remember her, no matter what.

Even though she was not with me physically, she always would be.

She pulled out my hands and saw the watch. Seeing her face right now, I could make out that she was embarrassed by the fact that I was not taking off the watch of Heather's grandfather.

I held her hand from the other, from which she held out my right one and took the velvet box. "It's beautiful, but I am genuinely wearing a watch that is close to my heart."

"Who gave you that?" she asked. I wanted to lie, but my heart said no.

Should I?

Should I?

Should I?

NO.

Moments passed, and without any breaks, I said, "It's from Heather." Her mood changed, and jealousy started dripping from her face.

"Okay. Let's go then." She slammed the box into my palm and fastened the seat belt across her.

She looked frustrated, but I tried to avoid confrontation from every instinct I had. I continued to focus on driving. The ride was going alright, and I was still driving.

Finally, we both decided to go to a restaurant, which was on the outskirts of the city, and it took us twenty minutes to reach.

As soon as we reached, I told her to hold on until I got out of my car and opened the door for her. Even though she was impressed by my gesture, she was still angry with me for not taking off that watch, and neither did I want to.

I snuggled her in until the waiter showed us our place to dine. She looked at the menu but ordered nothing. I knew it was bothering her, but I still asked, "What's going on? You seem a little upset."

"I am upset. I like you, Hades, and if you haven't noticed it by now, then it's obviously because of Heather. I know she is important to you, but where do I stand?"

"What do you want me to do, then?" I asked her. I had to.

"You have to choose between Heather and me. If you choose me, then you have to leave her; otherwise, I wish for you to be happy someday in the future," she said, and I was still staring at the face which was not ready to stay back from the statement.

I AM FUCKED UP!

Chapter 20

Hayley

"Why are you so envious towards Heather?"

"I am not envious towards her. It's just," I humbled, "It's just that she has always been your top priority when I am your girlfriend."

"She has been my best friend for a long time now," he defended.

"Hades, boys and girls can never be friends. Either one is in love, or the other doesn't approve of it," I stated. "See, Hades, I'll be very honest with you. I never had great relations with my father, and maybe a part of me is still hung up on it," I completed the sentence as shock belied his defensive voice.

He placed his hand over mine to comfort me and asked, "Something you wanna share? I am all ears if you feel comfortable."

I locked my eyes on him before I started with my past, with a sigh.

"I was a child when dad started bringing this girl home who was lower in post than he was. She had dinner with us most nights of the week. She was way too young, and I never seemed to have much of a problem with her until she left." A tear slipped away, and my voice cracked. "Whenever she used to leave the house, my mom and dad closed the gates of the room, and only yelling voices came through. Sometimes the breaking of glass, or you know, doors creaking. I would just go up to my room, close the door, clutch my knees together, and cry for hours."

As I was leaving, not leaving any part behind and reliving every flashback,

"The most miserable part was that every morning, I used to notice something in my mother. Like she was beaten up or, you know, choked. She used to be one of those people who used to smile even when the worst was yet to come, and seeing a person like this cry in front of you was a lot to take. My dad never once apologised for what he did to her, but yeah, he did say sorry to me for ruining the night's sleep."

Crying and sobbing, I completed with a broken voice,

"After some time, everything was back to normal. Just now, they weren't sleeping in the same room, but still, I was happy that there wasn't any kind of chaos. Then, one Sunday morning, dad came into my room and said that he was leaving my mother and getting remarried to a young woman. That time, I realised that she wasn't just a friend. She meant more to him. He left my mom and took custody of his money. Never, ever since have I seen my mom."

He wrapped his hands around me and consoled me as I said, "Even when he had a family, she was his priority. I feel the same. Even though I am your girlfriend, Heather is your priority. And that does, in fact, bother me."

While rubbing my back, he said, "Well, I am so sorry, Hayley! I never knew you had gone through so much in your past. If you had shared this with me before, I would have understood," and nodded his head before resting it on my shoulders again.

I detached myself from his warmth and tilted my head upwards with teary eyes. "I was never a bitch, Hades. But I really do like you, and there are few people in your life who make me seem low. I am not saying anything except the fact that I just don't like her to be around. If she will be, then you might have to let me go," I finished off with my final request.

Mission accomplished. I got myself into thinking, and that's another arrow to her ego. I pushed out all my emotions and tears in one go while hugging him tightly for the second time.

Chapter 21
Heather

"We wish you a Merry Christmas,
We wish you a Merry Christmas,
We wish you a Merry Christmas and a Happy New Year,
Good tidings we bring you…"

My hand was on my neck and elbows, touching my knees as I swung from one side to another, feeling this song.

The song was still going on, and I looked around the room to find everyone dancing and vibing. I felt kinda happy to sit around with my friends on the holidays like that and enjoy.

Joshua was sitting right next to me, and his sarcasm was going out of the line. I saw around, but I couldn't get my eyes on Delilah or on Hades. I hope they weren't planning to kill each other.

Both of them arrived with me to celebrate this occasion, and I couldn't get hold of both of them. Not one of them answered or replied to my texts, so I left them. It had been thirty minutes. I was sure they hadn't left the party because the car keys were with me.

I asked Joshua, but he had no idea, so I went to Chase, who was currently dancing with his new fling - I guess. I didn't want to disturb him, but he might know where they are. I walked over to him and tapped on his shoulder, "By any chance, have you seen Delilah or Hades?"

"I think I saw them going upstairs to the terrace. They were waiting for the Christmas fireworks and went up to watch them. We were all going to join them later. You should just go and check there once," he replied.

"Okay."

I looked for the stairs that led up to the terrace. When I finally found them, I quickened my pace to reach there, and by the time I climbed up half of them, I heard a glass break or something similar. I went towards the door, which was closed but not locked.

I knew it was wrong to eavesdrop, but I had to do it.

"Are you serious?" Hades sounded irritated when he spoke.

"Hell yeah, I am. You are abandoning her for what? A slut you barely know." Delilah was sounding more annoyed.

"You better talk to her with respect, Delilah, before I forget that you are a girl."

These words weren't making much sense as I didn't know the crux of the fight. Who was Hades defending? I had no idea whom they were talking about.

Both of their voices were sounding like they could murder each other.

"Hades, what are you going to do? Are you going to rape, hit me, or push me off this building? I suggest you do it; otherwise, I will be the one taking the first step," Delilah provoked.

My eyes widened with shock, which was running into my veins at that very moment. If anything had happened here, I would never have forgiven myself.

Both of them were important people to me, and they are actually threatening each other's life right, so I barged in immediately.

"What the hell, guys! Why are you guys here and fighting about something I don't know of."

"Are you going to tell her, or shall I?" Delilah pointed her index finger back and forth.

"Stop it, Delilah," Hades said with his eyes closed, showing the emotions that he just wanted to get out of here.

The finger pointed back at him when she said, "Your one lovely best friend here who is standing in this amazing outfit, who said he wouldn't go to Greece without you, who said he is going to be on your side forever, who said that the sound of you just existing makes the sense of the world is abandoning you for Hayley, the bitch he met for like two months ago. Forgetting the fact that you are the one who introduced them."

My eyes filled with rage but touched my cheeks with the droplets. My face was flushed. I heard this, and it broke every inch of my heart because I couldn't tell him that I liked him. I was waiting for the right moment, but there was no point.

I wanted to hold him and tell him that I liked him all along. I just never wanted it to be noticed.

I searched for his eyes and gazed inside of his soul to check, "Tell her, Hades, that's not true," my voice broke.

My eyes were still pouring out water, and when I walked towards him, he held his head down, not being able to hold the power of my stare or perhaps the truth.

I walked towards him slowly, pronouncing every word. Sentence I could think of, "Tell me, Hades, she is lying. Tell me she is joking. Tell me you guys are playing a prank on my patience." I grabbed his collar and shook him.

I just wanted to know that this fight was a prank on me. On my patience.

"All of it is true," he told me.

My hand dropped from his shirt, and I felt my 206 bones cracking into smaller pieces. My heart felt like a hundred pounds there, and I was not able to hold on to the truth that I had just heard.

I was going home, still trying to speak the whole sentence without breaking myself and crying into the depth of my own self. "Are you coming?" I faced Delilah with my teary eyes.

"I'll be out in five. Meet me outside." I told her while controlling my emotions.

As enough of me stood there listening to it, I turned towards the door and started walking when a sudden jerk helped me up. I turned back and saw Hades' fingers encircled tightly around my wrist, hurting me.

"I guess mentally hurting me wasn't enough; now you're also physically hurting me."

He loosened his grip a little bit so I did not get any grip marks on my body or to reassure me that he wasn't hurting me.

"Leave me," my calm voice took over, even though I just wanted to scream.

I made a point by jerking my arm from his captivity to set him free, but it wasn't possible. "Hades, leave the fuck out of me alone. You go your way, I'll go mine." He didn't let go of my hand; he was begging for me to at least listen to him, but I was too mad to do so.

I made my arm free from his captivity when he tried to hold me again. An instant fuel of rage came through, and I slapped him.

Ohhhhh no, shit, shit, shitt. Never should have laid a hand on him. My inner voice kept crawling back into my head.

As I stared in shock and avoided the situation by asking Delilah to meet me downstairs, I turned around and barely walked out of the terrace when I heard Delilah say,

"She never ever used her hands on anyone, no matter how angry she was or how much she was filled with hatred for someone. What you did was beyond explanation.

I really hope that slap put some sense into your mind and made you remember that she isn't the villain of your story. Well, I guess I need to leave, but keep your head hung like that and think what you did just now. And was it worth it?"

I took a pause in my steps. She took a pause in her words.

"If the answer you are looking for is yes, then I can't help you," she completed.

After listening to this, my eyes went into a blurry vision, and I couldn't see anything through the watery vision.

The tears kept shedding onto my cheek, but I still opened my car in a hurry before anyone spotted me. Delilah came soon after, and I just knew that in this condition, I couldn't drive a car, so I passed her the keys to drive me back home.

She started the car engine and told me to let it out, but I couldn't until I was out of this area. My eyes shed tears, but I didn't burst out by then.

She took the left side of the crossing when it was supposed to be straight for our apartment. "Where are you taking me?"

"To somewhere I know and somewhere you might like," she replied, "I can't let you go home in this condition."

For the whole ride, she played some of my favourite songs to cheer, but obviously, a lot was there to overthink when my own best friend or the person I am in love with just decided that I would never be part of his life.

She stopped in the middle of a jungle and told me to get out of the car. She held me close while turning on the headlight of the car. When we took a stride, suddenly she hugged me.

I burst into tears, hugging and crying to her, knowing that if it hadn't been for her, I would have committed suicide by now.

"Let it out."

Sobbing and crying, I completed every sentence I wanted to tell him, and I couldn't.

The worst part was that she was going soon, and I was gonna stay in the same school with Hades because he wasn't. I would have to see him every day, and the fact that he left me for some girl who he barely knew for a few weeks.

Chapter 22
Delilah

It was nine in the morning. I was having cornflakes and milk for breakfast before hitting the gym. Chase was sitting right in front of me at the breakfast table, reading a newspaper while having grilled cheese sandwiches and a cup of joe.

He stuck by Heather's side since the breakup. One of us always stood with her if another one had to leave.

We filled the breakfast table with all sorts of food that we could think of. Croissants, breads, eggs, different flavoured juices, and coconut chocolate cookies - her favourite.

The door unlocked.

We could see Heather coming towards us. She was wearing an old night suit, her hair held up by a clip, her pale face, dark circles from all that crying, and her emerald eyes turning crimson.

"Hey, Hon," we both said simultaneously, overlapping each other.

She gave us a slight nod. Not saying a word, she opened the fridge, took out the bottle of cranberry juice, and carried it with her to the bedroom, slamming the door behind her.

Meanwhile, we just eyed each other. We thought she might sit with us and have breakfast, but none of that happened.

"Oh my God. Has she slept at all?" Chase raised his voice and asked while looking at the slammed door.

"Nope. It's seven nights in a row," I told him. He sighed. "I mean, she finally stopped crying yesterday and went to the terrace, but then she found one of Hades' beer bottles." I pointed towards the bottle on the counter.

"Ouch," pitying our friend got broken like we never expected. "So, what are you gonna do about this mess?" He gestured, pointing at the bottle and the door of Heather's room, "And her?"

"Well, my first instinct is to kill Hades and then tell him that whatever he is doing is not good."

"Are you going to talk to him?"

"Yeah, of course. What choices do I have?" It was a question; I wasn't only asking him but also myself. "I know they are too interdependent, and I also know both of their egos are too big to admit it."

He nodded. He didn't say anything, though.

"I'll go to him after my gym. Will you be here in the meantime?"

"Hell yeah. I was thinking of taking her outside, to a park or maybe a club."

"Ohh, for the love of God, take her. If she IS ready to go." She has been refusing everything. To eat, to drink, to enjoy, to go out. Nothing has been working, even though we tried to make her laugh, but she ended up crying more.

Looking at the time on my phone, it's late. "Gotta go, sweetheart. Take good care of her." I gave a quick kiss on his cheek and walked out of the house, grabbing my essentials.

I was walking around the campus looking for Hades. I found him at the football field, sitting on the stairs, watching the game.

I walked over to him. It took me ten minutes to reach him. The ground perimeter is five hundred metres. Acceptable distance.

I sat near him on the lower stairs. "What happened? Why are you sitting alone?"

He hung himself, positioning his hands from his knees to the stairs. "Just wondering what it's like to live a normal life."

"You were living one. It just got complicated."

He turned to me. "How do YOU know? Do you even know what it's like to choose between a girlfriend and a best friend?" He snapped and faced the field again.

"Let me make this simple for you, Hades. You are missing her," I shrug my shoulders with a little on nod on the side. I just unveiled the truth that he might be trying to avoid all this time. So what if she misunderstood. Aren't they adults? They should be fixing things and sort it rather than sobbing about it.

"I certainly am not." He said. He sure is a child. Maybe similar to Heather at this point. Irresistible of the fact that they still love each other and can't seem to get them out of head.

"If you didn't miss her, then why is there a cup of cranberry juice on your right side?" I took my eyes off the field and glanced towards the cup at his side.

"Because it's good," he clearly lied to me while sipping. He placed his elbows on his knees again, pointing his hands in the field direction, putting all his weight into it.

We let time pass, and the wind sunk us.

"I still remember how you asked her for a date. You went to her and-"

"Bought the whole store," he completed my sentence and chuckled. "I remember that. The best way for real."

"It was a dick move," I laughed at him, and so did he. "But you know, I knew it in that very moment when she laid eyes on you. Not even then, but when we were both volunteering. I knew it then and there that maybe she could move on because of you."

He said nothing.

"You also know that whenever she trusts someone, she does it with her whole heart. The same goes for her hatred. Now you have given her the biggest betrayal of the century, ending up with her having some serious trust issues."

"I mean, I never wanted to leave her, but Hayley left me no choice."

"Just ask yourself, was it worth it? If not, I am here for you, little boy." I stood up, patting his shoulder, and was about to leave.

"Delilah," Hade shouted.

I turned back to him. "Hmmm?"

He was in the same position, except his face turned to me. "You are not angry with me for what I said?"

"On the eve?" he nodded. "No." I shook my head. "I am a little angry with you for ending things with Heather this way, but you will get your senses back soon."

"I am really sorry to you, kiddo."

"I am sorry too for what I said. Just do me a favour, Hades; if you don't want Heather in your life, don't barge in hers either," I completed. "I'll not be here for her soon."

He said nothing.

I thought for a second while walking away to tell him one last thing, "Whatever happened was fucked up. For seven nights in a row, she has been crying in her bed alone, and finally, today, she stepped out in the fresh air. I hope you understand."

I had my certain reasons to make him stay away from her if he was not ready to own her. She was already miserable and if he comes and goes back into her life, it will only just traumatized them more and more that they could imagine. Might on to that level where Heather won't be able to move on or find love in future.

For sure, I didn't want to see her go through that phase. This was already being unbearable yet I am managing somehow. I don't really know how but all I know is that, either all of them get their act straight or leave one-another presence.

I left the field soon after and later on texted Chase to ask where they were.

Chapter 23

Heather

I only came to this club because of Chase. There's no way I was in the mood for a party. Chase went to the bar to get me a few drinks.

Oh, I saw, Delilah. Wondering where she had been all afternoon. "Here you are," she said while sitting next to me on the club couch.

"Where were you?" I yelled. The music is so loud that I can hardly communicate with her. Sure I know why I hated parties. Still no one can top the Christmas party chaos.

"Nothing, just went to the gym and then at mom's."

"Ohh."

I noticed Chase placing four shots of glass in front of me. "Tequila, baby!" He's drunk. I should be the one doing so. "Cool, Delilah is also here," he slides the glasses to both of our sides. This party animal needs to be stopped. Oh dear, I am already on the edge to grab myself, how would I take care of this creature when Delilah leaves town.

Delilah and I gazed at each other. I picked up the glass and gulped it in one go. Another bowl of sliced lemons passed by, carried by Chase.

It's been so long since I partied. Two hours felt like heaven from the pain I have been enduring. This random boy was dancing well with me for about twenty minutes.

The song stopped, and I went to my best friend sitting on the couch. I saw another glass of shot and drank it. "Hey, dude, that was our shot," a voice told me.

My vision was blurry, so I couldn't really see anything. "I am so sorry. I'll pay for it," Delilah's voice carried from my side, even though I could see her sitting.

Delilah carried me to another table, and I drank the first drink I found there. I didn't care what I was drinking; I just knew that I needed it.

"What the hell is up with her?" the boy's voice sounded.

"She's thrashed," Delilah defended.

"Delilah, the love of my life. She doesn't know, but every time we hang, she's healing the wounds she never gave," I told the boy and flattered myself on the couch.

"Enough for today. Let's go home," she said, picking me up and lightly slapping my cheek three or four times to get my eyes to open. "Call him."

I woke up with the smell of peppermint on my side, inhaling it as I tried to open my eyes. The shock went through my stomach, the realisation of slowly sobering up. This wasn't my room. IT'S A HOTEL ROOM.

Damn it.

A hand slipped on my bare waist, pulling me to a body. Oh my God, I am wearing only underclothes. *Where are the rest of my clothes?*

I could feel the coldness of his touch against my body. Even though I was wearing delicates, I could still feel his abs. What did I do yesterday? And with whom? I turned my body around, and I felt a heart attack.

"Chris," the words just slip out of my mouth.

"Yeah, babe. Glad that you're awake," he said as he opened his big brown eyes, and I remembered why I had fallen in love with him before. After all, you never forget your first love.

He took his hand back from my waist, climbed out of the bed, and quickly put on his shorts. "Why are you here? When did you come?"

"I came to New York yesterday."

"Why?"

"For you," he said.

"What - For me?" he nodded. "Why me?"

"Why don't you dress up, and we'll go downstairs, eat breakfast, and I'll answer all your questions."

"WHAT?" I can't believe my ears from what I heard. Still processing.

"Yep," he took a bite from the scrambled eggs he ordered.

"Why?" I asked, in total shock. I wasn't able to answer; I still muttered.

"Because they want the best," he said. He wants me to be a model in a music video. Not only that, but also the show-stopper of his new collection. As if that wasn't enough, he told me that magazines want me to.

"I don't even know about this field or industry. There is no way I am going to survive here, and I have no interest in becoming a model."

"Believe me, you have everything," he eyed me up and down. "Your face is perfectly symmetrical. So is your body."

I opened my mouth to say something, but the turmoil in my head made me shut my mouth again.

He placed his hand over mine. "Listen, I am not forcing you. I just want you to think over it. It's a once-in-a-lifetime opportunity." He looked at me with his doe eyes as if he were asking me to think about it deeply.

Brushing him, I nodded. "I'll think over it." I took a sip of the mixed fruit juice, which was undoubtedly bad. "I wanted to ask you one more thing."

"Ask."

"Did we-" I pointed a finger back and forth to both of us.

"Yes, we did." A smirk showed up on his face, and I remembered the little child that he still was inside.

Officially, I lost my virginity.

Chapter 24
Heather

"You know, you don't have to drop me home. I can go by myself."

"I am not letting you go all by yourself," he told me as we were making our pace to the car. I stumbled at the door because if I opened it, I knew what I'd be getting myself into. "Heather," he snapped me out of my imagination.

"Yeah," I replied to my name.

"Sit in the car."

I opened the door, and I got in the car.

It's a forty-minute drive from his hotel to my apartment building. We didn't say a word to each other yet.

Not even out of curiosity, I couldn't gather up the courage to tell him that my first love was my first, but he was not quite what I wanted right now. I didn't know what I was going to say to Delilah or Chase. Both of them will be waiting for me at home.

"Heather," he called out my name again.

"Yep," I turned my face towards him to find him already glaring at me.

"I am sorry. Whatever I told you when I moved to Singapore, I know I hurt you badly." My lips pressed.

I was remembering the fact that I loved two boys in my youth. Both of them hurt me, except one wasn't a coward because he was true about what he felt, and the other was the biggest coward of all who left me for another girl.

"It's okay. It was two years ago. It's ancient history now."

"No, it's not okay. I had no right to say those things to you when your feelings were true all along."

"Let it go. It's okay," he shifted the gear.

I matched his gaze when he was looking at me. "Do you still feel it?"

"The feelings?" I asked.

"Yes."

I wanted to tell him about Hades, but his hopeful eyes were searching for a different answer. "I don't know, really," he said. He didn't say anything for a while.

Twenty minutes went by, an awkward silence. We didn't speak with each other until we reached my place.

Chapter 25

Heather

First day of school.

I was still standing in front of the mirror for over an hour, checking myself up and down continuously. My eyes fell on my shoes. It had been weeks since I had stepped in school with these shoes.

I wouldn't have even thought to go to school today if it wasn't for the important meeting that was to be held by teachers.

Even though I was satisfied with my uniform, I still had a few doubts, and all of them came back to only one person: Hades.

Delilah was gone.

Chase had been with me since I just couldn't handle bringing him into this hideous school. I mean, he had been in charge of the house after Delilah was gone because I had no power to take over myself. How could I have ever done that?

My phone rang again. I checked, and it was from Chris. It had been a week, and I have been avoiding him ever since that incident. I know why people go for friends with benefits.

"F**k and leave. Sounds a lot better."

Always choose that over continuous calls or clinginess. I wanted that but with someone who doesn't want to be mine. Chris might not be someone who I would want that with, and for him, I mean more to friends; hence, my reason to avoid him was quite capable.

Every memory kept on coming to the back of my head. That smile, that tease, that lip bite, those big brown eyes. And that's only because Hades was stitched in every tissue of my body.

As long as I am with you, I am not wasting my weekend.

She ain't you, babe.

I ain't like other guys. I want you. I, Hades Ages Hawthorne, promise Heather Kades, in the presence of God, that my soul is for her.

I know she might trade me for a Subway Sandwich, but I never ever had a fake laugh with her, neither did she. I sure love my own company, but I will never leave hers because she makes me happier than anybody else in this world because... She is my Best Friend. She has been a shoulder to cry on for me in my ups and downs; I will do the same for her. If there is a possibility of another universe.

I lifted my gaze up and watched my emerald eyes, getting ready for a tsunami.

ENOUGH. I fixed my blue check skirt and the school tie. I wiped my tears off and went directly to the kitchen until I spotted Chase getting angry at his new fling.

People might not take this issue very seriously when they meet Chase, but he was a real player when it meant making guys fall in love with him. I should have taken advice, brah.

"I am just gonna go, guys. And stop fighting over silly things." I was sure Chase was the one at fault for real. He might have just told the guy that he was nothing but a sex toy, but I hope that one day, he finds something similar to what I felt. I want him to fight for it, unlike me.

Hypocrisy! I grabbed my keys and went straight out of the door.

No further discussion or talk happened on my way over to my car in the basement, and I drove off to school wondering what would happen in school today. I have already taken a lot of leave to be sitting at home.

I walked into the school and saw girls looking around, waving at me or whispering loud enough for me to notice but not hear the exact words. My intention was clear: I did not want to engage in further conversations with any of them. So, I went straight to look for my friends around campus, who obviously didn't exist.

Hades, friends are only what I have got, and today, for the first time, I needed them on my side, but they aren't here. "Hey!" I spin around to the voice that headed over from my back.

A pretty face came into view. She was dressed elegantly. Eyelashes were curled up perfectly. Mascara was done neatly.

No stains on her uniform. Shirt and skirt pressed. Shoes polished. She looked astonishing.

After viewing her up and down, I finally waved back and replied, "Hi. Do you know me?" I pointed out.

"Who doesn't know you, bro? But the question is, do you know me?" I don't, actually, but I kept on trying to remember that face, which was impossible to figure out when my friend circle was extremely limited, especially in school.

One of them is gone, and the others left me the day Hades did, I guess. "Sorry, I am having a hard time remembering you," I said in response to her question.

She looked at me and gave me a cup to hold. "I am Kimaya. I have been transferred to this school, and Delilah sent me here." I stood there, stunned. "It's cranberry juice. Your favourite."

I came to my senses. "How do you know it's my favourite, and how do you know Delilah?"

"Online is vast." That's all I needed to know. For a second, I panicked over and went into my nerves when I felt she maybe would take Delilah from me.

"Anyway, nice to meet you, Kimaya," I said as we shook hands. "Can I ask you one more thing?"

"Yeah."

"Why are these girls waving at me and staring at the same time?" I looked around to show the people who kept on repeating their actions as I looked at them.

Without a second thought, she wrapped her arm around mine and started walking towards the corridors. In the midway, she uttered, "These girls heard that there is a new opening beside you since Delilah is gone. Everyone wants to be with the school queen."

"No way I am."

"Anyway, want to go to the library. I heard it's another favourite thing of yours." The excitement as she spoke made her eyes glittery. Damn, this girl knew everything about me. I am kind of scared but pleased, too.

A chuckle escaped from my lips. "Sure. Before we go to the library, I just want to go to the sports room to drop off some forms."

She nodded, and we headed off to the sports room.

Mr. Sports was telling me about the more request forms. As soon as my conversation with him was over, I looked at my side and saw Kimaya looking at the sports memory board.

This was the idea of our former teacher, who used to put up photos of her favourite students and some candid photos of us playing sports.

I was looking at this after a long time since the school's swimming pool shifted to another building. I didn't come here as often as I used to.

"See this. Isn't this you and Hades?" she pointed at the picture, which was taken approximately a year ago. We, both standing in our red school jerseys, were wearing each other's birthday numbers.

I nodded with a soft smile, but Kimaya noticed.

"Sir, we need one more basketball for the third court," a similar voice at my back. The third court equals the Hades court. I turned around and watched Zara talking to Mr. Sports.

Zara in shorts.

I whispered into Kimaya's ear as I pulled her, "What is she doing here?"

"Babe, whom do you think she got admission for here?" That question felt like an arrow to my heart. I can't believe her. I guess it wasn't enough to take him from me; now she is trying to make my school hers.

"Anyway, let's get out of here," I said. I had no intention of facing her.

We walked out of the sports room and soon entered the school building's fourth corridor. Walking past everyone, we finally found out more about Kimaya.

Hades

There's no way I was going into that stupid class of mine. It was super boring, and to bunk this class, there was no option but to ask our sports sir to create a fake practice if any teacher asked.

Walking down the third building, the topic that Hayley changed her school because of me was still going on. I saw her in the field with those shorts that were trying to move up from her backside and that high ponytail swinging.

That got me blushing a little bit, but it made my friends drool over her, too. Stepped up over the fourth building on the campus, and I saw two pretty girls walking out of the sports room from fifty feet away.

They kept walking nearby us, and it sucked that today was a serious meeting in the auditorium, because of which I wore this stupid uniform.

No wonder it was the best way for the school to make us wear our school uniform once a week.

The distance between us and those girls was getting shorter. We kept on getting closer. "What the fuck?"

My mouth flung open when one of those girls turned out to be Heather, my own Alpha. She kept on walking.

My friends glanced over to my direction and planned to run away, but my feet didn't stop. She finally lifted up her gaze twenty feet before me, and emerald ocean met the brown boat which was meant to drown in it.

In the background, everything started to fade away, but our feet kept on moving. We crossed each other with a poker face.

The face in which we both know that we are dying without each other inside, but those eyes never leave each other.

She walked past me, still, eyes locked in mine and vice versa. Our heads turned, and our eyes were not getting tired of looking into each other's souls.

Mine is asking for forgiveness. Hers asking for love.

Finally, at both ends of the corridor, we turned our heads back to our conversations with the same eyes. Just this time, a tear shed, and I wanted to throw up.

Chapter 26

Heather

I never anticipated that an eye-to-eye *conversation* that just happened could make my heart shred into pieces.

"Is it easy to give someone love and not get anything in return?" a voice came through from my side, and I see Kimaya waiting for an answer.

"One-sided love has its own bloody power. The most beautiful thing it possesses is that, unlike other relationships, it doesn't divide the love between two people," I replied. "Only I can claim the privilege of this love."

Leaving the conversation in between, I slipped my hand into my pockets and took out my phone. Without any second thoughts, I called Chris after that deep, eye-to-eye conversation with someone who hurt me.

Broke my heart into a billion pieces.

He picked up my phone, and my last words before cutting the call were,

"I'LL DO IT."

Chapter 27

Hades

I have had no updates of Heather recently. Kind of wondering what she's been doing all day long. Without her, anything I do is not exciting anymore.

I see Hayley sitting across the table. On a date with me. Then why am I still wondering about Heather? Is there any part of me that still wants her? I felt a sudden guilt rushing through me. One month away from her felt like the Earth is breaking down into pieces.

"Oh, this is super amazing. Taste this," Hayley said while turning the spoon filled with Blueberry cheesecake towards me. *Realising I am with someone else.*

I opened my mouth, and she fed me. "Yes, it's good," I mombled.

"You look low. Has something happened?"

Yes, something happened.

You made me lose my best friend, the girl that my family loved, the girl I cherished, the girl who's ghosting me,

haunting my dreams, and the girl I am hallucinating to be with every moment. You made me lose my girl, my Alpha.

I snapped out of imagination into reality. Heather is not the one with me right now, Hayley is. "No, everything's fine." My voice lowered in a way that I can sense myself lying. I look down at the croissant, which I don't feel like eating anymore.

My phone started ringing and vibrating. It was Joshua.

"Excuse me, I have to take this call," I told her.

"No problem."

I excused myself from the table and walked out of the café. The call was disconnected by then. I searched his name through my call logs to dial again until his name showed up on my screen.

I picked it up.

"What?" My voice sounded harsh.

"Have you seen the cover page of Elle Delight?"

"Elle Delight? What's that?"

"You are damn stupid. It's a magazine like Vogue, except in this magazine, girls get themselves photographed in lingerie or bikinis and other stuff."

"Why would I see that? And why are YOU seeing that?"

"Bruh, let me send you the cover page of this month." For whatever reason he called. It must be stupid. It should be.

After all I was receiving a call from Joshua about some fashion magazine.

My phone buzzed. He is still texting me like a stupid person when I am present at this very call. I opened the chat and downloaded the photo he wanted to show me.

My eyes widened from shock. The cover page was a photo of Heather. She is not in a normal outfit that includes a slit, but she is actually in a white bikini, lying on top of a hundred brown teddy bears. Her hands postured in a way that enhanced her every inch and flat tummy, looking as curvy as ever.

Make-up was done and everything. Red lips, eyes with a smoky touch. Then, the realisation filibustered, and my face shrunk.

"Did you see it?" Joshua announces on the phone to check if I am still alive.

"Yeah, you have called me... to show this?"

"Of course, dude. Today is her first show. Guess who the designer is." for god sakes, this guy was truly the gossip feeder. Ain't he a man who supposed to be focusing on his career but whenever I talk to him, I feel to be around a group of women sharing stuff to bitch.

"Who?" I asked.

"I said, guess who, babydoll. So, guess." Swear to God, if he was standing here with me, I would have murdered him right now. This is not the time to play GUESS WHO.

"Are you telling me, or do you want your ass kicked?"

"Why so angry, man? Jesus Christ. It's Chris Knight."

Chris Knight. Her former love. First love. From whom she moved on. Tattooed herself that she will never love him again. Oh, that guy needs an arse-kicking.

"Hey, babe. Everything alright?" a soft voice followed from my back with a sudden touch on my shoulder. She slid her fingers from my shoulder and directly came into my sight, looking at me worried.

"Hey, listen. I might have to call you back later," I told Joshua and disconnected immediately. I turned my eyes towards Hayley, and I told her, "Nay, everything is fine. Just some work came up. Come, I'll drop you home."

Heather

"Heather, you are next," Avery told me.

Avery, Chris's show manager, took a final look at myself in the mirror. I asked one of the volunteers to get me the heels that I was supposed to be wearing in this show.

I was wearing those lacy heels and walked towards the backstage. I saw Chris standing there already.

I walked towards him, showing him the make-up and the dress - a black bikini designed by him, to be exact. "You look gorgeous, honey." He gives me a peck on the cheek.

I smiled. "Thank you. But I seriously think you should change your show-stopper. I am not the right fit for it."

"Someone get her the bathrobe," he ordered the girls standing, who were waiting for a task while ignoring my words.

He cupped my face and told me to relax. "Don't be nervous. I know you are made for this, just take a deep breath in." I inhale the rest of the air present between us. "And out." I exhale.

The girl brought him the bathrobe. He covered it and told me the instructions, leading with it. I heard every sentence, every word in that sentence.

"Thirty seconds on the cue, Heather," Avery said from the back.

The lights dimmed. It's all dark. The triangular-shaped entry turned black. Only I could hear the song that was being played at the back. I felt the adrenaline rush through me.

"Now," Avery instructed.

I stepped into the triangle, and all the lights of the gate turned on, blinding me.

Chapter 28
Hades

After spending my whole evening here, I couldn't believe I was sitting in a fashion show with my ex-best friend. I spent approximately around a thousand bucks trading just a ticket with a stranger.

It's the biggest moment of her life, and I don't be certain of myself that I actually came here to give her loads of shit about this.

I don't know what happened to me. I was the one who left her, and still, when I saw the board while entering this fashion show, it said-

Mermaid Waves by Chris Knight,

feat. Heather Kades.

A sensation burned me up. I was about to leave when the place went all dark, and I could only see the media flashing lights.

I guess Heather stepped in because the music playing in the background grew louder. The lights of the entering frame removed the darkness of this room.

The beat dropped, and the light popped up, open, all focusing on her.

She walked on with a black bathrobe on the ramp. It was her main character moment. The audience focuses on her. Everyone is looking at her.

I am looking at her.

Her pace working phenomenally on those lace heels. Sliding my gaze up, I see her still in a bathrobe. Halfway to the ramp, she clung onto it with both hands. Another beat dropped, and she removed it.

She looks stunning. I couldn't take my eyes off her. Damn, she's making me regret every hellish decision.

It is a two-piece set. The upper bra was black and laced on the side. Not forgetting the fact that it was push-up and combined with braided rhinestones. The strap was not the kind that is tied at the neck but was taken all the way to her lower back, like in a bra. There were only two hooks at the back on the braided rhinestone, criss-crossing each other.

The lower part is simply black, except for those that resembled hipster shorts. They were cut on the sides in a landscape rectangle on both sides of her waist.

Her hair exquisitely falls down her back. Her eyes, not intending to be broken, are so focused.

I see the bathrobe cuffings still clinging to the wrist, and the rest on the floor following like the veil of a bride.

Excruciating pain was felt in my body when I saw her with those thick thighs, and I wanted to stab every man's eyes in the room, but my hands are tied to this possibility.

"Ladies and Gentlemen, the most awaited person of the show. Please put your hands together for Mr. Chris Knight." He walked on stage and took a stand next to Heather, hugged her, and then started walking to the front again for the photos.

His hands on Heather's bare waist actually made me realise how much I hated this guy.

"I don't believe that a guy like him can make this," the girl sitting next to me said.

"I don't believe the girl who's wearing this," I said. The music is getting louder, and so does the audience's applause.

"Ohh, she looks GORGEOUS. So does he. It's a kind of turn-on for a guy about these boys that are into fashion." I am into fashion, but that doesn't mean I out gay myself.

I leaned towards her. "He can't be more gay!"

"Huhh??"

"He can't be more gay!" I told her again.

"I can't hear you. The music and applause are too loud." oh my gawd, I didn't realised it until now of much I hated chaos. All the parties I have went to were all because of a simple reason. Heather.

"HE CAN'T BE MORE GAY!" The music stopped, so does the praising when I said it. Everyone's looking at me. I was looking at everyone.

I see Heather and her murderous green eyes looking at me as if she could literally poke my eyes with those high heels she is wearing. I could see the anger flow through her body.

It took me some bribes and a lot of threats to barge myself backstage just to meet the woman I was here for today. It was worth it because when I saw her conversing with some ladies, her eyes were sparkling.

She hasn't changed her clothes, except this time, her bathrobe actually has a knot tied around her waist. She is talking to a few models and hugging them as I heard those girls adore her.

She saw me, standing there in my normal outfit. She excused herself from her party and walked towards me. I ain't ready to take this right now.

"Hey," why am I the one starting a conversation?

"What are you doing here?" she asked, her hands crossed around her chest, trying to be harsh with her words.

"I….I….. I came here."My words were being humbled but another man's presence just hurts my respect of not being able to speak in front of the woman I love, more and more.

"You slayed, babe. Didn't I tell you that you would?" Chris, fucking Knight, came into view. He fucking hugged her and kissed her on the cheek. She looked into his eyes and smiled.

That smile was mine. I just want to rip that fucking head off his. This was getting unbearable. And unbelievable. What could she possibly see in the gay styled guy?

He saw me when he held out his hand. I poured out mine, "Hey, man. Guess you are the man who said about me being gay," he said while shaking my hand.

Embarrassed about that moment, I just nodded and narrowed my eyes in an apologetic way.

"Hey, don't be embarrassed. A lot of people mistook me," he said while grabbing Heather by her waist and pulling her closer. He looked into her eyes. "As long as my girl is here with me, I am fine."

Your girl. She is my girl.

I just want to make him forget that the smile he is giving right now will never exist after The present day.

A girl came into sight and told him, "Sir, the reporters are outside."

"Okay," he said. "Gotta go, man. Great seeing you here tonight." it wasn't for me certainly. Perhaps I would have given him a decent chance if he wouldn't have broken Heather in the past. But that guys was no good.

He was looking for my name, so I gave him "Hades." I just wanted this guy to leave us alone as soon as it was possible. I wanted to talk to her alone. Leave things in a better way.

"Hades. See you around." I surely would not. If I would, there would be another headline coming in my head that *Chris Knight was beaten to death by Hades Ages Hawthorne.*

He walked away, and I waited until we couldn't see him anymore. Heather started walking away as well. I followed her around until her steps led to her vanity van where she turned immediately to face me.

"Hades. Just leave, okay," she told me.

"Are you seriously dating this guy?"

"It's none of your business." even thought she believed it was none of business but everything I am was because of her. So yea, everything she does in the range of my reign, it is my business.

I grabbed her wrist, not letting her go. I got slapped once for this, and it was worth it. "Why him? Why is it always him?"

"Mind your own business."

"I know I did wrong, Alpha. I know you don't want to be back with me, but just-" I took a pause and exhaled the air. "Just be my best friend again." I know I was at fault, but I needed her forgiveness as well in order to move ahead with my life. I made a promise to Delilah, yet Heather's forgiveness is what I seek. Maybe she would never be able to love me back as I do, but at last, I want her to be close to me again.

She put her other hand slowly on my hand like silk. Her eyes filled with water.

"Hades,Hayley created a space between us that YOU and I can never break," she told me.

Reading into every word she said, I let go of her hand, and she went inside the vanity. She disappeared. My heart was slaughtered once again with her choice of words.

I walked into my house, knowing full well that this day couldn't have gone any worse.

My phone got switched off in the middle of the show due to low battery. I walked into my room. I plugged the charger into my phone. Meanwhile, I changed my clothes and told my butler to make dinner.

By the time I came back to my room and switched my phone on, I saw thirteen missed calls from Hayley. I saw my text and Hayley were the most crossing twenty-plus messages.

I opened the chat, and there it was, filled with abuses.

Hayley: Come on, you've got to be kidding me.

Hayley: you lying piece of shit.

Hayley: you mother**er. You went to her show. Didn't you?**

And so on…

How the fuck did she know now? Cursing my life at the very moment. Every time I feel that this day could not go any worse, universe proves me wrong by bringing more chaos I imagined of.

There was also a link to a tabloid, and I opened it. Shocked by reading the headline.

'Hades Hawthorne, the heir of one of the richest Greek families, indicating that Chris Knight is gay?'

Cursing under my breath, I now understand how the hell she knew. I run my hands over my face and through my hair. I don't want to deal with this right now.

I scrolled into my call logs and Face Timed Delilah.

Ring.

Ring.

Ring.

She picked up the call.

I saw darkness instead of her. "It's five in the morning in Greece. Hell, you know that. You lived here, bitch," she said.

"First of all, I can't see you." I saw some movements in the darkness, knowing it's her. I hope she is turning on the lights.

She switched on her night lamp so that her face could be a little visible. "Now?" I nodded. "Tell me the reason you called for."

"Is Heather dating Chris?"

"What?"

"You heard me." she obviously heard me thought her mind would work slow to process it given the fact that she just woke up from her night-night sleep.

"Hades. I asked you one favour before coming to Greece, and what was it?" Her eyes were sleepy, as was her voice when she said it.

I know what she said. "If I am not keeping Heather in my life, then-"

"DON'T BARGE IN HERS EITHER," she yelled. "One rule. One promise. One favour. And you can't keep any." Her voice was firm.

She narrowed her eyes while looking at me as if she was going to kill me. I saw her nostrils flare up. Both of the best friends have some kind of power to scare the living daylights out of me with their murderous gaze.

"Is she dating him or not?" I asked her again. She was annoyed. Oh my god, when did this mattered to me so much that I couldn't let my friend sleep without knowing.

"Yes. She is with him now," she admitted and broke me. Saying it like everything is normal, but it's FUCKING not. "I thought you got that today when you were in the show." certainly this is the era of my life, where I want to punish myself for letting her go.

"How did you know that I went to the show?"

"I read about it in a tabloid that the heir of the richest families in Greece insulted Chris Knight on his show." *Oh my God, if she had read it, then my family would have read it by now, too. I wanna hang myself.* "I'll handle this drama tomorrow. Good night."

She disconnected on my face as I kept looking at the screen. It took me two minutes to realise she was no longer on the call. That bitch.

Anytime soon, I was waiting for a call from my family to arrive, shouting at me.

Chapter 29

Heather

"I hate her, truly," Kimaya spoke as we were both sitting in the cafeteria alone, and Hayley walked past us with her little trio of Joshua included.

No matter how much you give to a person, it won't be enough. "I do, too." I ain't afraid to speak what I have in my mind now. The gossip about what happened between Hades and me has been all over the school.

It wasn't a shock for people who were unaware of this that he showed up at my show last night. If it wasn't enough, he also called my technical boyfriend gay.

Not everyone loves Hayley, but many heads turn around for me out of sympathy. My best friend moved to another country, and Hades (my best friend and also the person I loved) left me, too.

Distracting ourselves from other than Hades was a choice that Kimaya and I adopted. We might not be on the top anymore, but she is still a bro. "You miss her, right?" Kimaya blurted out.

For a minute there, I thought she was talking about Hades, but she said 'her.'

"Delilah?" she nodded on the verge when I spoke. "Yeah, sometimes. If she were here, I wouldn't have to deal with people trying to sympathise with me so they could be friends with me."

"So, when is she coming back?" I don't even know the answer to that question. I haven't talked to her since the news about the fashion show. Yeah, we texted a lot about the stuff that went on, but the topic of visiting never came up.

"I guess in what the fuck." A beverage has just been spilt all over me. I looked over to the person who held the cup, and the urge to say 'it's ok' spiralled out from my body. "Damn it, it's all over my dress."

I grabbed the tissues, so did Kimaya to help me out cleaning them, too. Wiping off, my gaze lifted up, and I saw a smirk on Hayley's face. *She did this intentionally.*

I see my surroundings and feel people's gaze on me. There are gasps, there are laughs. Antagonistic are her eyes when she leaned over to match my height and said, "I am sorry." The smile never left her face, but I guess from today she won't be left to survive.

She started to walk away, but I was in no mood to let this go. In no time, I followed her and gave her a tight push. She moved around to match my eyes and smiled like nothing had happened, "If it bothers you so much, just take it off. It's not like you are going to get embarrassed. You did it before."

She looked me from up to down, referring to me as a whore. "Anyways, I wanted to ask you one thing," she continued, "How does your dad feel about you dressing like a slut?"

Everyone's eyes in the room were on us, with another gasp on their face. "I don't know, but your dad likes it," I said in a way that surely made her face just in a way to cry in a few seconds.

Another gasp went around the hall.

And she took offence and came in front of me and slapped me. The eyes were on us, and my focus went directly to Hayley's head following my hand. I held out both her hands with one of mine and used the other to grab her hair.

That was an advantage when I pulled her hair and slammed her head into the nearby table until she bled. As riveting as it was, her hands got free, and she reached for my hair, which was currently open.

It wasn't much of some help, but she tried her best to pull them until I took the glass plate and banged it against her head.

Let's see how much she can smirk. "I told you long ago not to mess with me. I thought of you as my friend, and what did you do?" I finally left her hair and thumbed; she fell on the ground with a weakened body.

I folded my legs and told her, "Next time, think before you mess with someone." I took a stand and brushed off my hands. My eyes gladly awaken when I just showed people my psychotic side. It was unknown to almost everyone.

I look over to Kimaya and give her the signal to walk away with me. I see her smiling, knowing damn well she was proud of me.

It took us a minimom of two minutes to leave the cafeteria and make our way to the infirmary. No doubt, I need a bandage after this fight. I hurt my finger while slamming her on the table.

I entered the infirmary and watched Mrs. Kakkar sitting on the chair giving first aid to one of the students in the Junior classes. After she finished, her attention moved towards me when she spotted me in the room. "Hey fighter. How come you are here?"

Fighter. A nickname she gave me after my right arm was fractured in last fall's swim meet, and I still decided to swim. Since then, she and I have been in casual touch. "Hi, Mrs. Kakkar. I just needed a bandage and something to wear off my headache."

She opened up the bottom drawer of the desk and took out a box. Through the translucent surface, I saw the bandages among a few other medicines. She tore off three bandages and handed them over, "Here you go, sweetheart."

I grabbed the bandages in my hand.

"I suggest you lie down, sweetheart because your face looks pale." No wonder I beat up a girl, and my dress is also in cranberry juice. My hair is a mess, and I am tired.

"Yeah. The headache is quite severe."

"You want to go home. I can write that for you."

"Can you do that?" I asked.

"Obviously." No wonder she was known to be the coolest teacher ever. I have only heard that about her, but today I saw it.

I asked Kimaya to join me. I guess it was the first time she was coming to my apartment. I can't wait to reach home and call Delilah, as well as ask Chase to run home fast so I could spill them this stuff.

It took us about twenty minutes to reach our apartment from the school's parking lot, including the traffic. We used the elevator, and I opened the door wide open for Kimaya to enter.

I showed Kimaya around the apartment but couldn't find Chase or his boyfriend. I was telling Kimaya about him when a call interrupted us.

It was Delilah. She usually calls at this time when I am in school, but not so long ago, it was the same routine since there was no whatsoever intention to go to school.

I picked up the FaceTime, and Kimaya and I filled her in with the details. Her shock-happy face lightened up my mood, but another call overlapped. It was an unknown number.

I answered Delilah's last question and told her that I would call her back later. I redialled the recent missed call.

"Hey. Is this Heather Kades?" the person on the other side of the call asked.

"Yeah. This is her," I replied.

"We saved you as the emergency contact for Chase Omen. Mam, I am sorry to inform you that Chase Omen was found behind an alley, all beaten up and bruised." His eyes were filled with water, and Kimaya asked me in an expression about what was happening. The person on the line was still speaking, "We found him with three ligament tears, a broken leg, and rib. He was bruised-" and she went on describing the injuries.

The only person in the town I cared about, and he was beaten up to death. Without wasting another second, I drove off from the street to the hospital. Kimaya was with me the whole time, helping me to gather up while I was breaking down.

We reached the hospital in no time. I asked for Chase's room number instantly as I stopped at the counter.

We ran towards his room, and I saw his name outside the room. Another heartbreak spread throughout my body. My nerves were breaking, and my brain was clearly not working. My hand stumbled upon the knob, but still, the little courage inside of me was shattered as soon as I pushed the door.

I saw him lying with drips and fractures on the bed, and I was horrified onto the floor in seconds. I could literally see his bruises with my blurry eyes, and for sure, he wasn't stabilised yet because he hadn't woken up from the noise of my screaming and crashing to the floor.

Kimaya helped me once again to gather myself when I took a seat on the stool next to him and slid my hand below his, not grabbing it with too much force.

177

Chapter 30
Heather

After spending twenty minutes with him, I had to leave him in Kimaya's care. I have been asked to collect Chase's things from the reception, and I had to inform his family as well.

The nurse finally joined my presence at the reception after quite a wait. I grabbed the bag from the nurse's hands and started moving back towards the room.

I opened the bag and found everything that belonged to Chase except for that one pouch with a ribbon. I took out the pouch from the bag and closed its chain.

I entered the room to watch Kimaya asleep on Chase's hands while he was holding it. I looked closely at those two. Both in peaceful sleep, resting in each other's comfort.

I placed the bag on the couch below the window and seated myself next to it. I unzipped the pouch…

There was a letter in it. Without any second thoughts, I tore the envelope to unfold the small piece of paper, which only stated,

Guess you were messing with the wrong person, as well.

My eyes got numb, and this turn of events could never hurt Chase, or that's what I thought.

Chapter 31
Hades

I never thought that I would ever show my after-school place to Hayley, but my friends didn't talk to me before bringing her here.

It was a classic two-story room reserved for me and my friends. It had all the classic games, a dance booth, a pool table, and more. It was an after-school relaxation place. Play stations were on the table in front as we sat on the couch. No girl was ever allowed in this area until Heather.

This place was a secret, only open to me and my friends.

"Oh well, he deserved it. SHE DESERVED IT," I heard Hayley saying it to me while I was defending Heather as she was putting compression on the bruises.

"Whatever you did was wrong," I said. I looked around and saw my group shaking their heads in agreement, "I told you not to mess with her, but you did it anyway. Including Chase was never part of the plan."

Everyone in the room was once known to Heather, and they knew the fact that Heather could be harsh when it comes to her stuff. She didn't fight for me to Hayley; that doesn't mean she didn't know how to put up with one.

"I don't agree to your terms. Neither do I work on it. It was my choice." Her words were the fuel to my anger. I couldn't, obviously, handle much of this nonsense, so I just lay back with my hands on my face.

I heard the passcode pinching sound from the side of the door, and the next thing I knew, Heather barged into our space.

"I told you to stay away from me," she said, looking at Hayley and striding fast.

I took my stand and said, "See, Alpha, we've got it. Whatever she did was wrong."

"Hades, don't involve yourself in something in which you weren't invited," she recited without once looking towards me, and it didn't take less than a minute for her to come around us and grab the collar of Hayley.

Without any thought, my hand landed on Heather's neck and slammed her directly into the wall. In my defence, I did it carefully. Her gaze filled with rage, and mine filled with the urge to protect Hayley, crashed into each other.

"Don't touch her," I said.

Her body went still, and she was close enough to make me realise that her heartbeat had slowed. Her nostrils were flaring, and her crying voice could be heard inside her.

Her broken voice said, "Did you ever fucking love me?"

Those words and tears slipping from my eyes made me reconsider whether I ever loved her. Her eyes locked with mine, and I knew that I was not in love with Hayley, but I was definitely in love with her.

"I was never in love with you, Alpha. It was just a game with you," I told her with a straight face that I put up. It was hard not to break into pieces at that very moment, but I kept holding tight to my inner self.

Nevertheless, I let loose my hand that was, at the moment, wrapped around her neck. "I hope this person doesn't change. It's easier for me to hate you this way." Tears slipping continuously, she continued her words, "Don't ever change back to the person I fell in love with."

Her lips tightened, and her body shook a bit before those wet eyes closed and decided to disappear with her physical self. I know I could never forget her, but I will try.

Chapter 32
Heather

Another two months passed. The beginning started in a blur of wet eyes, work, and hospital visits on Chase, but now he was also up and about and started going out often.

I was late on my periods for weeks. It happened to me all the time, but not for more than three to four days. It was weird because I was late for three whole weeks this time. My day couldn't have started better with this thought puncturing into my mind.

Due to my menstrual cycle being off for such a period, Delilah suggested that I should take a pregnancy test. I kind of explained to her that maybe it's the stress because we all know that it causes hormonal imbalance. Either it's the lack of knowledge in her or me.

But still, to my doubt, I bought the pregnancy kit on my way back home from school. I was sitting in the bathroom, waiting for two minutes to be over and show the result.

Constantly, things were wandering in my mind. *What if I was pregnant? Will my career be over like other models?* I ain't Gigi

Hadid; I will be fine after having a kid! *What will society say?* Aside from that, I was just eighteen, so technically, it would be considered a teen pregnancy even though I was an adult.

I looked at my watch, and it was time.

I pressed my hands together and closed my eyes to pray not to be pregnant.

It took me another minute to open my eyes and notice the test, only to find the two red lines on it and congratulations on the display.

Shit. No, no, no, this can't happen to me!! I

I sat on the floor disappointed while staring at the test in my hand.

"I got fucked," I reminded myself. Literally that's how I got myself here as well.

It took a few minutes of my time to think rationally, and with that thought, I got my clothes to change from my wardrobe. I took a shower instantly and ran off to the gynaecologist.

I needed to confirm this news. I must do that as soon as possible.

"Congratulations, Heather!! You are eight weeks pregnant," the doctor said with a smile on her face, and I fell back onto my seat, my hands holding my head.

I was having a headache and an urge to vomit at the same time. I spaced out in my own imagination, and the doctor kept on rambling about some medical terms to which I was unknown.

I was looking at my file and she had the copy of the same to which she was flipping pages. She captured my attention as she said, "I am assuming you are keeping the baby to term," she lifted her head and saw me with a look of disappointment on my face rather than the joy of being a mother, "otherwise, D&C is the only option. You have come too far along with your pregnancy."

I was screwed at that very point. She held my hand in hers and pressed it gently, "Take your time, sweetheart. And it's okay to be scared."

I nodded.

It was a cold night, so I came onto the balcony when Chase wasn't at home, and Chris wasn't spending his night either. I looked downwards at my tummy and moved my hand around it a bit.

Babies were never part of the plan I was building. Maybe at the age of twenty-six, I would have considered, but surely not at the age of eighteen.

I wasn't much of a smoker, but I did have two or three puffs backstage of the show when I was too nervous. And I knew where to find one.

I walked to the backside of the balcony and entered Delilah's room through the sliding glass door. The perk of knowing her for so long was that I knew she must have hidden the pack of cigarettes somewhere safe.

I turned the lights on and checked in every drawer, but I wasn't able to get a hold of the pack, though I did find a lighter.

On that note, I saw that there was some space behind the television in her room. It was attached to the wall, so I couldn't really see what was there.

To that note, I slipped my hands at its back, and I felt something of a box. I guess I found it. I tried my best to get a hold of it again, but before I could grab it, it fell on the floor.

I picked it up, turned off the lights, and moved back to the balcony.

I stood against the wall, took a cigarette out of the box, and lit it up. I took my first drag, and the flavour of peppermint filled my mouth. I sank into it, and that night, I sat on the floor rather than on the chair.

The night didn't end there because soon after, Chase entered the home and came to the balcony looking after me.

He joined me from the same door through which I first entered. "Hey," he said, looking at the fact that I was smoking.

"Hi," I replied.

He sat next to me in no time and leaned on the wall behind him. "You seem sad," he confronted. Was my face being to obvious with the life altering situation. I guess it was.

As a matter of fact, he wasn't wrong anywhere. I didn't know where the future was taking me. I was someone who wanted to control everything, and for the first time, I was feeling that life was taking me to my fate, and I just replied to him, "Well, something happened."

"Truth clock or Dare unlock?" he said.

We built up this phrase when someone was upset. If one chose the truth clock, it meant that he/she wanted to share. If dare was chosen, it just meant that the other person would slam you with the stupidest dare possible, and you would do it to distract yourself from the thing you were stuck on.

"Truth unlocks," I took another puff and said. The eyes that were fixed on the view finally moved towards him as he was doing the same. "I am pregnant."

His eyes widened, but he kept his voice much lower than I expected. He took a deep breath in and exhaled.

I diverted my eyes back to the view and rambled on, "I killed off the only plant I had at home. How will I take care of a REAL HUMAN BABY?" I had my point of view, "This baby is going to hate me. And how will I support it? I am just a model, and my career is now over, so basically just a student. And what will I say to Chris? He barely started loving me again the way I wanted. I am sure he wouldn't want to be a father at the beginning of his career." I looked towards him again and asked, "What should I do? Tell me."

To my frustration, he questioned, "Are you ready to be a mom?"

It took me another two minutes to stabilise myself with the wind that was slowly sinking us into more comfort, "I don't know, man."

"Baby, we can't tell you what to do. Only you can decide that," he explained. "But I am with you no matter what you decide. And if you choose to have the kid, it will have the best aunts and uncles in the whole world."

I took the last drag and threw it away as my eyes started to fill up with tears. "I am absolutely clueless, Chase. For the first time."

He pulled me in for a hug instantly and started rubbing my back with his hand. "You are going to be fine."

Chapter 33

Heather

"Mom, have you seen my choker anywhere?" I shouted under my breath while trying to find it in any of my drawers or Delilah's, "Kimaya needs it."

I reached in the morning only to meet my parents once before the weekend got too busy. Dad would join us for brunch since it had been a long time since we all had a meal together. I actually wanted to let them know about the circumstances I was in for a week.

For now, I pulled the drawer attached to my study table and rolled my chair around, this time with ease. My eyes fell on a file, which was certainly different from the others. It seemed like a hospital file until I pulled it out of the drawer and found out it actually was.

I flipped it open and noticed my mother's name on it: AGE-17.

Only one thing came as an outcome, and that was MY MOM HAD A BABY before me.

She was running upstairs as the sound intervened on the flight. "What do you need, Heather?"

"What's this?" I held up the file and asked, "Were you pregnant before me?"

"Heather, I can explain," she said. Oh so it was true. It wasn't just some fake file or made up file. Oh my god, how did I not look for this before. The revealing of the truth just began, I might not know what the universe will bash on my face again with other truths.

"There's nothing to be explained. It's clear from what I have seen," I stated while opening the file. "Well, guess the lying gene runs in our family." It was obvious that I had a sibling, and she never cared to let me know about him. "Does dad know?"

"Heather, whatever you must be thinking is wrong," she objected.

"It's not. Better off alone, I was. Oh my, how much of a dumb ass I was that I thought I shouldn't share about my pregnancy since I was only eighteen, and here my mother was, one step ahead of me when she got pregnant at seventeen," I revealed as I threw the file on the table and ran downstairs.

She followed behind me, and somehow, due to my pregnancy hormones, my tears became visible. I was drowning in my own sadness, for I don't know what reason.

Obviously, my parent's house wasn't big enough for me to run off freely, so my mother caught hold of my hand earlier than expected, and my feet came to a stop at the backside of the lawn.

Tears were rolling down my cheeks, and I was sure that she heard me crying. She pulled me closer as my body moved towards her; she pulled me in for a hug.

For the first time ever, I hugged her that tightly as if I never wanted to let her go. I was bawling on the verge of not being able to breathe, and every tear was falling onto her shoulder.

She rubbed my back in the circumstance of consoling and did it until I stopped crying.

I was sitting on the floor, taking the support of the wall, and mom was sitting right in front of me. My eyes were down towards my hands, and mom's gaze was at me when she asked, "So, do you want this kid or not?"

I said without lifting my eyes."Aren't you angry with me?" It was the guilt. Of humiliating her. Of not let her know the truth. Of keeping it to myself. Of being a hypocrite.

"You want this kid or not?" she asked again.

"It's not as simple as you think, mom. Without marriage, a kid, and that too at the age of eighteen," I protested with my lower and broken voice while my eyes never left the sight of the floor.

"Want this kid or not?" Damn. She was not budging off of this question, and I just wanted to cry more after it.

"Talking to you is quite difficult, mom."

"Heather," she called out, and my eyes finally met hers. "I know you must be thinking that whatever you did was stupid, but believe me, I was once dumb and stupid. I had you legitimately at the age of twenty-nine when I had all the support in the world. But when I was seventeen and pregnant with your brother, there was no one on my side except Rachel."

Rachel was Delilah's mother and, I guess, was the only one who stood by my mom's side when she had no one else. "I wasn't dumb for being pregnant, but I was dumb for working on society's terms."

My soaked eyes and half-blurry vision took every ounce of the experience she was sharing with me today.

She cupped my face and wiped my tears off with her thumb as she continued, "You remember what I once told you at the beach." I remembered that advice. I had totally forgotten about it. But the support and that words were amazing. It gave me hope.

To the memory, which I had forgotten about, I closed my eyes.

"Where are you taking me, mom?" I said as I was walking, not knowing where. My mom's hands covered my eyes, and a little sand was getting into my sandals.

"Just trust me," she replied.

To her trust, I was still walking down wherever she led me. After walking for two hundred metres, my legs felt cold water touching them. In only a few seconds, she removed her hands, and my eyes welcomed the most beautiful sunset I had ever seen.

The most mesmerising scene I could have imagined was right in front of me. Waves were gently rolling and crashing down against my feet.

Gently, my mother turned me around while kneeling down. "You told me there were girls at your school who were giving you a hard time for having emerald eyes, and because of that, you wanted to change the colour of your eyes."

"They called me a snake," I corrected her as she matched my gaze.

She scratched my forehead with her index finger and took hold of both of my hands with hers. "Calling a snake is not a bad thing. Snakes are the prettiest reptiles of all. They are smart as well."

"They didn't say it as a compliment. They meant it in an insulting way," I replied.

She took a sigh, "Kiddo, we meet thousands of people in our life. We only remember the faces of three hundred and the names of a hundred. Among them, there are fifty people we call for celebrations or funerals. And finally, there are those ten people who know our ups and downs before we do. We can be blunt with them, and they will never, ever leave us for it."

I nodded.

"So, think of your ten people, and even if they are fewer, it's no issue."

I opened my eyes.

"Remember now?" she asked.

I nodded.

"Society is dumb for setting such a standard. I tried my best to make sure you didn't get caught up in it, but you did. And it's better to get out before you tangle yourself more." Another tear fell off, and she wiped it. "Kiddo, you had five people at your back then. Who are your five now? Don't think about what society will do or think about it. Think how those five would react if your happiness lies in it."

She went silent, and I thought of my five.

Delilah,

Mom,

Dad,

Chase, and obviously,

Hades.

"Whose child is it, by the way?" she asked, the very question I was scared of. "Hades, is it?" The shock spiralled into my body, and my eyes widened at his name. This wasn't how I imagined to tell her but what else can be done.

I shook my head.

"So, Mr. Knight, it is."

I nodded.

My tears were finally stopped when she asked again with a smile on her face, "Want this kid or not?"

"I do. I wanna have a child, but with the one who actually wants one," and that's all the words that came out of my mouth with tears. It was understandable enough for my mom to know how I actually feel about Chris.

To my reply, she stood up and helped me to do the same, "Let me bring you cranberry juice, then we'll discuss this further."

As she was about to walk away, I called out, "Mom."

"Hmm?"

"Can you tell me more about my brother?"

She looked into my eyes and soul simultaneously. She showed a bit of a smile on her face and said, "His name is Nick. I gave him to a family in Singapore who couldn't have any children. I just wanted my child to be secure financially, and as I said, I was just seventeen years old when I had him. The family he belongs to works in the mafia somewhat."

Another shock just came, which my body couldn't handle. Is he a rich man? Damn I might be related to someone who was as rich as Hades.

"But he does call me sometimes."

"He knows?"

"Yes. Before meeting your father, one day, I was incredibly low in my life, so I called the family and got in contact with him. He was only six years old when I flew to Singapore to meet him. I loved him dearly, so when he turned nine, his parents told him, and since then, he calls once or twice a month."

"Does he know about me?"

"You might not know this, but he protects you a lot because his connections or threats are not good."

"Can I call him?" I questioned. I just wanted to be sure if I could contact him and if he would feel okay if I did so.

"Sure, kiddo. I'll give you his number," she reminded, "after all, he is your brother."

Chapter 34

Heather

It didn't take much time for mom to digest the news. It was four in the evening, and I postponed all my contracts since my parents booked me an appointment for an abortion.

I told her my concern and shared everything that had been going on recently with my mom. It was understandable to her that I wanted to have a child, but with someone I actually wanted to have one with.

She was calm about the whole situation and shared it with my father at the right time. He wasn't angry either. He also told me about the issue of mom's teenage pregnancy and how mom informed him on the first day they started dating.

In my current time, I was lying on the bed of an abortion room, and a nurse was by my side checking my pulse as well as my blood pressure.

"Take two days' rest, and everything will be fine," the nurse said, wrapping up all the kits in her blue uniform. "The doctor is going to join you shortly."

She left the room, and as soon as she was gone, my eyes fell on the glass window of the room. There was a beautiful view outside the window; all the buildings were so huge. I looked around only to notice some of the cutest baby portraits on the wall in front of my bed.

I sat up straight and poured some sanitiser on my hand from the table next to me. As I started rubbing my hands, I noticed the wallpaper on the walls, which had little cartoons on them that I grew up watching.

I looked upon myself in the green dress of a hospital patient and thought, what was I doing? Ain't this a murder? Born or not, its heart is still inside of me.

I slipped out of the bed and put on the slippers that were on the floor. I opened the door and walked outside. My legs felt like they didn't have much power in them to hold me. It was the guilt that was rushing through my body, which didn't allow me to just lie on that bed.

I saw my parents outside, seated on the chairs that were placed in the lobby. As soon as they detected my presence, they stood up and made their way over to me as I was trying to walk.

"Are you fine, kiddo?" my mom asked.

"Why didn't they give you a wheelchair?" a question from my dad overlapped.

Mom asked again, "How does it feel? Is it over so soon?"

I lifted my head up and looked into both of their eyes, waiting for an answer. "I couldn't do it, mom," I said, while my voice broke. I continued with my words, bawling, "I just couldn't."

My mom hugged me at that instant and patted me slightly on my back, "It's okay, kiddo."

I hugged her tightly, with my shoulders resting on her shoulder. "I just couldn't manage to murder a child, especially my own. I am too scared."

"Nothing to be scared of baby. You were always our princess, and we are here to help with the baby," my dad continued while patting my head. "Two months, three months, or six months. As long as you need."

I closed my eyes and tried to calm down and be happy with myself for the first time that I would be a mom. I would try to be the best mom like my mom was to me.

Chapter 35

Heather

My current life problems were so overwhelming that I found ways to escape. When I wasn't bound by my contracts, I was working on my academics. I kept myself as busy as possible to forget what had happened, to forget Hades. Apart from that, I was going to have a baby.

My day was spent in either the library or in my studios to avoid the one person I shouldn't be with. On the other hand, Kimaya developed a natural bond with Chase.

Delilah tried to check on the baby and me occasionally. I usually rang her up with a heavy heart and swollen eyes. The thing that hurt me the most was Hades calling her, too, which burned me up, but I had no right to stop that because no matter what he did, he was still a good friend to Delilah.

I still remember the time when Delilah called him at night and shouted at him because he laid his hands on Chase and me, the most trusted people for Delilah. Though never once did she mention him about my pregnancy because I wasn't comfortable with it.

It had been a week, and I had not yet told the father of the baby, so until then, I was keeping quiet.

I was casually sitting in the library, currently reading a classic novel, to be in an imaginary world, escaping my present problems. Involving myself in someone else's life issues gave me a release. It was my Alice in Wonderland. Another reason to be sitting in the library was because this was the only place where Hayley never visited.

"There are more classics in the second story, section eight," I lift my gaze from my novel towards the voice and direct it towards Miss Singh, our librarian. She was quite a teacher. Her taste in books and novels matched mine. She looked at my novel and continued, "You are about to finish this novel, honey. The school has received more books from Shakespeare. I guess you can take a look at them. You might love it, " she smiled and winked at me. I reciprocated with a smile and a nod.

She placed a hand on my head for a blessing and moved ahead to another table. I separated myself from where I was seated, closed my book, and placed a bookmark. I grabbed my classic in one hand and stepped onto the stairs after a minute.

When I reached the second storey, it was only shelves as long as my eyesight goes. I searched for section eight and looked for the shelf on which I could take another book by my favourite playwright, Shakespeare.

People do say that he was overrated sometimes, but I disagree with them because writing epic plays at that time was awesome.

Every line that he wrote made sense, but if you look at its explanation, it defines a totally different meaning, which is even more exciting.

Even my favourite fictional character, Aaron Warner from the Shatter Me series, loved Shakespeare, and his lines impacted Aaron so much that he had to get a tattoo of that line.

The shelf above said

SECTION 8

SHELF-D

Shakespeare's plays and poems.

Found it. Yay.

I was going through every book title, believing that I couldn't find one that I hadn't read. This could be a shock to people that there was no bigger fan of Shakespeare than me. He was a legend.

I finally found an unrecognised titled book on the above shelf. I stood on my toes and tried to reach the upper part of the shelf to get it, but it was not possible due to my height.

I was nearly leaning on the shelf to reach for it, but the mission failed. I tried again, and this time, I tied my hair at the back.

I was about to reach it when my knuckles touched the palm of another person whose fingers were currently touching the same book I was trying to get my hands on. "I guess you need my help," a thick, dominating male voice behind me said while overpowering me with his body.

I turned around, and his bare chest covered my entire view. In my defence, I wasn't looking at his chest until I saw his white shirt unbuttoned, which gave me a perfect view of his slippery abs.

I slowly lift my eyes up from his chest to his neck, and then to his sharp jawline. I was having a great time until I saw who was behind that body because it made my eyes pop.

"Here you go, Alpha," Hades said with a voice that I didn't recognise. He made it up. So fake that I could literally sense it through his words.

He placed the book right between us while leaning on his one hand over the shelf, as I was against it myself. My face didn't change from its poker way, but my windpipe sure was choked after a fire that was pulled between us during that very moment.

I remember, the last time when we were this close, he told me that it was just a game with me. I swear to God, if he changes at this very moment, I am going to break his nose.

I slipped the book into my hands from his and left his space in ten seconds. "You didn't say anything," he said over to me when I started walking. "No, thank you?" he asked.

My footsteps stopped at the end of the aisle, and I turned my face to look at him with his soft eyes directed towards mine. We took a moment and kept staring at each other until

Kimaya spoke from my back, "She doesn't like speaking to people much now, especially when those people include you. So go and suck Hayley's dick now."

My eyes widened at the fact that she had just told Hades to suck a dick, especially his girlfriend's. My head spun back to her, and I tried to communicate through my eyes so she would not create a mess here right now. My pace started working its way back.

I touched her shoulder with two books in my hands and whispered, "Let's get out of here." Before she could say anything, I grabbed her hand, pulled her out of there, and went directly to Miss Singh to sign off the books and take them home.

Chapter 36

Hades

She left me standing. I was recalling every moment when she was in front of me. She had changed; she doesn't look at me the same way she used to. *It's killing me.* I had changed that beautiful soul into something that I could never imagine. My head spun at a headache that not only she had changed but I have also changed myself.

The fact that I went there to apologise and actually ended up asking for a thank you with a fake voice that poured out of me. *Am I that bad of a person?* Guilt rushed in.

If it weren't for Hayley, my hands would have never met her neck. Even when I pressed her against the wall, all I could think was to kiss her, that too, in front of my girlfriend. *She is my Heather. My Alpha. And she hates me.*

I never wanted her to leave, but life never goes according to plan. The Alpha I knew was the one who called me and gossiped about everyone for hours, and I, who was on the other side of the phone, used to get paralysed just by her voice.

She was gone. She was not the same anymore. *I have destroyed everything.*

My body was on fire and burning into ashes, every inch of it because I couldn't do anything. I was guilty of changing her into a person who doesn't say a word to anyone anymore. What have I done?

I shouldn't be thinking of her, but she crossed my mind every second of my day.

I pulled my phone out of my pocket and called my sister. She could be the only one who could help me with this.

The certain detail that Heather and I weren't together anymore hadn't been shared with her yet, but I had a feeling her reaction wasn't going to be a nice one.

"Hey," she said

"Hi. How are you?"

"Cut the bullshit, how much money do you need?" I know she had some burdens on her shoulders, but that was simply rude and upfront. Might I remind her of this. If she wasn't the elder one, I would have shouted by now, but that would have simply gotten my ass kicked in either way.

"What? I don't need money," I replied.

"So, why did you call?" for the love of god, isn't it normal for a brother to call her sister when he wants to let it out. What the hell is up with the world.

"I miss you." The problem was that I wasn't lying about it. I did miss her. If she was here with me all the time, I would have never done something that stupid.

"Really?" the shocked tone literally voiced over my head.

"Obvio."

"Well, to that, I say I miss you too." That 'miss you too' sounded more of a favour like *At least I am saying it back.*

"I want to share something, but you won't understand," I hesitatingly said that. I knew that she was going to get angry, and she knew that damn well too.

"Try me," between her strict voice, she said it in an understandable way.

I indulged her for another hour with the whole story. Meanwhile, I walked out of the library and went straight back to my apartment.

I was still filling her all about the details, while lying on my bed without changing my clothes. And today's interaction came in our conversation when she told me, "Hold on. Let me put this straight. You guys split over a girl."

"Yes," I confirmed. "You know, what the sad part is, that in a world where physical touches are normalised so much, I am craving for her emerald ocean eyes to look at me, for my heart runs a bit faster with her gaze."

"Hades, you know, why is your name Hades?" she asked a question that I never asked myself. This is a question that arose in my mind when I was in Greece but never vocalised. It wasn't that I didn't want to know or that my parents wouldn't answer; I just felt it was a bit dumb.

"Yeah. Mom named me after the God of the underworld because she loved him," I replied.

"No," those simple two words broke me out of curiosity when she completed, "Mom named you after the God Hades because he loved only one woman and was loyal to her." She took a pause, and here, I imagined her scolding me, but here she said something completely different, "God Hades loved Persephone, and how you talk about Heather and look at her can make anyone sure that you are in love with her."

I closed my eyes and imagined her hair getting messed up because of the wind. I am remembering the time we spent on the sea, not forgetting the time we spent in the cathedral and danced outside.

I spiked back to the present when my sister, over the call, said, "Maybe right now, you are thinking this girl, Hayley, something is for you, but believe me, from what I saw with my eyes, I am sure that Heather is your Persephone."

I didn't say anything because every word she spoke made sense, and I couldn't believe that I had been so dumb all this time.

"Hades," she called out and said, "Nothing is louder than the silence between a boy and a girl who would have been perfect together if just one of them put their ego aside and started a conversation. The ego is not bigger than love. Nothing can win over it."

She was right, but she deserved to know that I changed the soul that resided in her. After telling her that Heather had changed too, she told me one simple thing, "Weren't you portraying all this time that you hate her? She is doing the same because I felt that in the cathedral, she loved you as much as you do."

"Thank you, sis."

"Anything for my little bro."

She hung up the call, and I dialled Heather's number. My thumb was just above the calling option, and a notification popped up from my cloud.

I tapped on it, and the photos of Heather and me showed up from a year ago. I watched every video and went through every photo, smiling idiotically in every one of them. The smile that I saw was gone from her face in every photo. *Damn, these memories.*

I clicked on the liked video to open and see what it contains, and there it was: an edit of us slow dancing to the tunes of *I wanna be yours*. It also contained the video we posted on our Instagram and the videos of the beach in Miami where we went on our school trip. I hold on to those memories, my happy memories.

The times when Heather was always on my back while with a camera on our faces and I used to take her around on the piggyback ride thing. This made me realise that before calling Heather, I need to do something else. I went back to my call logs, and this time I called Hayley.

Chapter 37

Heather

I came home early from school. I didn't want to spend a single minute more on the same campus to avoid that one person whom I met today at the library.

Aside from that, I had one more reason, and that was Chris's celebration of his upcoming collection tonight. I had to be there since I was the one who was opening up his show.

I had my dress picked out, and right now, I was in my kitchen experimenting with new cuisine. Baby cravings were really weird. I wanted to have a taco for breakfast, and by the afternoon, I just wanted to try something new.

Chase didn't go to school today either, as he was busy doing something all night and needed to complete his eight hours of sleep. By the time Kimaya dropped me off at home from school, he was already awake.

At this point, I didn't have any kind of idea what he was doing in his room with closed doors. To cheer him up, I guess I had another reason to cook.

I was never a person who knew household work. My parents always treated me like a princess, and even when Delilah was my only roommate, she never overloaded me with kitchen stuff.

A spontaneous thought arrived in my mind today after meeting a certain someone that I need to learn to cook since I was going to be a mother soon. After Hades, every turn of mine took me to the worst outcome, but for the very first time, after a long time, I felt happy.

There was a glow on my face every morning, though I missed wine a lot, but it was worth quitting if it would be to bring this baby into the world healthy.

The door opened to Chase's room, and my focus changed. "Have you decided on names?" he said, barging into my *-everything is ok-* space.

I looked at him while scrunching my eyes and pouted my lips, "Well... not yet."

He was so excited as he leaned on the slab in the kitchen while I was cutting vegetables. "What do you think it will be? A boy or a girl?" he asked.

From the perspective of a mother, I had a feeling of a girl, but I wanted a boy. I don't know; I guess I lied before to Chase about not thinking of a name. There were a lot of names wandering around my mind, and this one specific name had a hold on my heart: Rayee. "I don't know," I said, "whatever it will be, I'll name it then and there."

A chuckle left his mouth. "So, how's mommy doing?" can't he just shut up about this baby puns. At first it was funny how he referred me mommy for the dominant one in the group but now this was getting annoying as I am pregnant.

"Craving for something I don't know myself," I informed.

The main door opened, and Chris entered our conversation, "Hey, guys."

"Hey man," Chase said to him, seating himself right in front of me on the other side of the slab.

I was still waiting for the oil to warm-up so I could fry some vegetables before trying this recipe that I found online.

Chris came around to my side of the slab, kissed my cheek, and said, "How's the baby doing?" and just looked at me.

My eyes widened at the statement in shock. *How did he know?* The fact was, I hadn't told him about the baby yet. I thought that I would let him know at the perfect time.

My eyes had their sight on his, and with doe eyes, he was asking for an answer to which I had no reply.

Chase noticed panic on my face, with sweat pouring down, and instantly had the idea that I hadn't informed Chris yet about my pregnancy.

Chris looked back and forth between us and said, "Are you ready for tonight? Didn't I tell you about the launching of new designs?"

Ease went over to my spin and then to my body. For a minute there, I thought he knew. I tucked my hair back. "Yeah. Yeah, you did. Something was just on my mind." One day, if I find that person who created these pun, he would be dead by my hands. That question gave me an heart attack until he cleared it out.

"Cool," he said, walking towards the opposite side of the slab and seated himself beside Chase.

"Want to eat something?"

"Yeah, sure," he said.

I looked on, on the other hand, and Chase looked back and forth between us. This was alerting as well for me that he might have just discovered that I hadn't told Chris that he is going to be a daddy. Literally.

Another thirty minutes passed while I was still working on the recipe, and Chris was engaged in a conversation about something related to his designs with Chase.

I suggested some ideas to put in, and both of them took my words seriously.

A call from Chris interrupted me as soon as I slid the plate into the oven. "I'll be back. I have to take this," he said, glancing towards his phone, and then headed out to the balcony.

The moment he left the space, Chase looked at me with his doe eyes. This eye contact damn made me nervous. I knew what he was going to say, but still, I asked, "What?"

"He doesn't know?"

"Nope," I accepted.

"Heather," his head tilted towards the side when he said that, with longing disappointment in me.

I pressed my lips and answered, "I know what you are going to say. That he deserves to know."

"Obviously, he deserves to know. He is the father of the life growing inside of you," he pointed out. "What do you think? You will cut out Chinese food and wine, and he won't find out."

"I don't want to burden him. It will just create more stress right now," I defended.

"What will create the stress?" Chris joined us again while walking inside the room from the balcony.

We both zipped our mouths, and I realised that one of us had to say something to avoid the obvious. "Nothing. Just this school paper that I have been putting off for a long time. The deadline is near, so I thought of doing it tomorrow instead of tonight since we have to celebrate."

He nodded and came around my side of the slab again. "Anyways, I have to go now," he kissed my cheek and hugged me, "pick you up at six," he said and walked outside the door, closing it behind him.

"It would hurt him more if he finds out from somewhere else." Chase made a point, and I agreed with what he said.

"For sure, tonight, I would tell him. Right after the party," I assured. "Can we eat now what I have made?"

"As long as it's good."

I put on my oven mitts, slid the plate, which held our brunch, and placed it on the slab. I served him with my experiment until he gave me the green signal that I could have this without making myself sick.

Chapter 38
Hades

I knocked on the door several times and rang the bell. The house was empty from what it seemed. The bouquet in my hands contained her favourite red lilies, and I couldn't wait to win her back. So many emotions running through me, I wasn't able to contain my smile.

It felt like forever to wait for an evening like this where I could ask her to be mine. *And this was it, it was my moment.*

In much anticipation, I rang the bell many times, hoping for her to open the door. I imagined her in a beautiful white dress with open hair, light make-up, and a slight smile on her face. *God, she is beautiful.*

Nobody answered the door for a while.

I checked the time, and it was seven in the evening. Where could she have been if not at home?

I called Delilah because she was the only known person I knew who would know where Heather might be at this moment.

"Hi," she said.

"Hey, I just wanted to ask, do you know where Heather might be?"

"Hades, don't do this again," a sigh left her mouth over the call when she completed it. "Please don't make me come back and break your face. Remember my promise."

I tightened my lips while she kept on reminding me of her promise, "I broke up with Hayley." The words poured out, and a silence took place instead of the speech she was giving me.

"What? Am I hearing you right?"

"Yes, you do. I broke up with Hayley," I confirmed.

"Why?" the stupidest question came from her side. Her best friend, sure, was dumb but fiercely protective towards Heather, but she didn't know that I obviously wanted her back. I broke up with Hayley for her. There, standing on the corridor, to ask for her forgiveness on my knees, to take me back, her Hades back. All in that moment, I wanted to know was the whereabouts of my future wife, my Alpha.

"Because no matter how much I tried to escape Heather, I can't, and now I don't want to either. SHE IS MY PERSEPHONE."

"I know I am going to regret why the hell I am telling you this, but she went to Chris's stupid party."

The jealousy intervened at my core, and all my words said was "thank you" to Delilah. He was surely the one person she loved in the past, but the reality was I am her present, and she was my future.

Chapter 39
Heather

"Chris, this party is so not my cup of tea," I said in his ears, with the speakers behind us blasting at full volume. I hated chaos. These parties were my thing. Dancing, drinking and chilling, everything was so similar to my liking yet I don't find myself comfortable.

"Give it a little time," he replied. "I get you don't like parties, but it's a success party." He doesn't know me well enough for sure.

There was a reason I stopped partying. I used to love parties, but Christmas one wasn't a great one. It sucked on every part, and still I was still in the party.

I nodded and went off to the washroom. I called Delilah, but she didn't answer. It was unusual because she always picked up my calls.

I mean, at parties like this, I always miss her. She was my pillar to hold on to. Even though I know Chris, I can't trust him with myself. I looked into the mirror, fixed myself up, and walked out of the bathroom. Chase surprised me when I saw him sitting in my seat.

He rose up and hugged me. "Bored?" he whispered in my ear.

I pulled back and said to his face, "Extremely!"

"So, let's do one thing. You sit here for another thirty minutes, and then I'll take you home," he offered.

I nodded, agreeing to his terms. Chase is the only one who gets the meaning behind my expressions. This party was nightmare to handle for another three hours. I might as well, tell about the baby to Chris tomorrow. When probably my head would not be aching.

I sat down, and Chase mixed himself into the crowd. I can't seem to find Chris either, so I just ordered myself a soft drink and sat down for peace in a place like this.

I saw a good-looking guy making his way towards me in an amazing all-black suit. "Hey," he said, "I am Jess."

"Hi, I am Heather Kades," I introduced myself.

"Of course, I know you. Who doesn't? I have seen every one of your interviews and your photo shoots." I mean, I am flattered by this admirer.

I got a negative vibe around him. I didn't feel very good, so I tried to keep the conversation as low-key as possible.

Chris and my news isn't out yet, so he might actually think I am single. Before anything happens, I should just thank him and leave. "Thank you so much." I grabbed my drink and got up.

"Can I have your number?" he said as soon as I was about to take my first step. His phone is in his hand, with the dial pad open.

"Sorry, I actually have a boyfriend." I turned around and felt blessed when I saw Chris on the dance floor. I pointed in his direction so the guy I turned down would be clear about who I was.

I see his face with a lower expression. He flipped his phone back into his pocket and moved back to his table. I glanced over there, and from what it was looking like, everyone was making fun of him for getting rejected.

I ignored it and Chris reached out to me in the meantime. He pulled out his hand. "Wanna dance, Miss?"

I slid my fingers to his palm and nodded. He yanked me towards him and held my spine. The song turned to a slow one, and we swayed ourselves into it.

After two or three songs, I was tired enough to sit back down. I was about to find Chase to ask him for a ride back home, but as soon as I opened my phone to call him, I saw a missed call from Delilah.

I called back in, hoping that she'd pick up this time.

Ring

Ring….

"Heya, girl," she picked up and said.

"Hey." the songs blasting in the background and people shouting at the top of their lungs made her voice sound muffled when I couldn't hear anything. "Let me go out because I can't hear anything."

I stepped out of the party and descended the flight of stairs in front of me for more peace. "Yes, now I can hear your pretty voice," she said to me over the phone.

"Aww. You know, a big party is going on, and I so wanted you to be here with me. I miss you."

"I miss you too, more than you can imagine," she replied.

Oh my God, someone just grabbed me from the back, and my phone slipped out. My mouth was covered by someone's hands as I was trying to fight with every power I held.

My legs are kicking non-stop, and the guy that I rejected shows up when I hit him right in the centre of his male part. He doubled over and slumped to the floor.

My mouth is still covered, and Delilah's voice is reaching me continuously, saying the word 'hello' to ensure about me.

I saw a security guard on my way from when Mr. rejected was still on the ground, and another guy still trying himself to fight me. I am so glad that the security saw this. "Wait. Wait. What's happening here?" he sprinted out the words.

Opposite happened, and I died from the lack of humanity when he held my legs up to help. Mr. Rejected raised me up from the ground and helped them to get me into the car, which was slid up on the side.

"Help. Help," I shouted at the top of my lungs when the hand freed my mouth. I am sure Delilah heard it, but the guy who was holding me back crashed my phone onto the ground with his leg just after.

They tied my body in the car with the seat belts. There was another person other than security, a guy, and Mr. Rejected. Constantly, my urge to fight was going on and on, and they were all holding me down.

They were still tying me up, and I was not letting them when the security punched me right into my face, and I started losing consciousness.

My eyes were dampening down, and the car was moving fast. Another punch hit me right on my face. "Call your boyfriend now," I heard one of them say.

The next thing I knew, Mr. Rejected (the first guy) spread my legs apart and used every masculine part to overpower me.

I regained my senses at the time when the car stopped, but my body had no energy at all to move or react. I bled all over and was given a lot of dosage in between. "Is she dead?" I heard my eyes not opening.

"Yeah, I guess," another voice followed. I held my breath for a bit to make sure they thought I was dead, and instantly, the car stopped.

In one quick motion, one of them picked me up and threw me out of the car, like one throwing garbage out of the house.

I tried to open my eyes and noticed, from my blurry vision, that I was thrown in the middle of the jungle.

A leather bootleg kicked me right onto my belly, and I rolled down to another road that was down.

After lying for hours and not being able to stand, a car finally stopped. A family was in it, and the driver and the female came out of the car in a hurry and comforted me in their back seat.

Not power in my words, I finally gathered up some strength and said, "Take me to -" and the next thing wasn't an address of a hospital that I should be going to, but was an address to Hades' house.

Chapter 40
Hades

I was worried. She didn't pick up any of my calls yesterday, and later, her phone was switched off. I did show up at the party and looked for her everywhere, but she wasn't present.

I spotted Chase and asked. He was the nicest of all, who didn't even give me a look while talking about her. Her boyfriend, Chris, was also there, but he didn't know either where she went.

"Sir, there is someone on our property. A girl named Heather," Mr Bolani said. He was my house caretaker, who was sent by my parents. I am surprised he forgot the girl who showed up at my house a lot.

"Let her in." Without hearing any more words, I went to the house door and clicked it open.

SHE SAID, COVERED IN BRUISES, "I WAS RAPED."

Chapter 41
Cicilia

"Was that Hades?" Aristos asked as he lay on the other side of the bed, shirtless, holding a classic book in his hands. It was weird that he could focus on both.

"Yeah," I confirmed.

I checked my last few messages as he continued to read. I was never very much fond of reading until he recited one for me in his own words. It was he who made me believe that literature was far more fun if it was explained by someone you loved dearly.

Our match was profoundly just an agreement between our fathers. I was forced into it when I wanted to pursue something much called a career, but in a society in which I expected to stay and present myself, I utterly disagreed. As such, I included my father as well.

Loved mathematics but was never allowed to pursue further studies because of the agreement that was in place. The only person who understood my concerns was Aristos. In every thought thereafter, he was present, yet there were paths of dreams that I was meant to follow but couldn't.

I looked at him and certainly noticed that, even with my concerns, he never stopped me from being who I am. He let me be the way I wanted to portray myself without other opinions and bickers that ran around.

"I had a doubt, certainly." My beloved husband punctured my thoughts as he spoke the statement while slamming his book down.

I glanced into his eyes and said, "Continue."

The lights were already dimmed until he turned the last lamp off on the nightstand before sliding his book next to it. He slipped the quilt over, and we both lay down facing each other.

"When we were about to be married, everyone told me about Hades being super introverted and how he likes his alone time," he smiled. "But what I have observed so far is that surely he isn't a private person."

I chuckled before I answered, "Hades is a private person. Actually, he was a private person. Even though I was the firstborn, he was the first boy, the first heir to the estate. I guess we have never heard his voice outside our house. He used to be someone who locked himself all day in his room, only coming out for dinners." I turned my neck and stared at the ceiling. "Then, one day, he finally asked if he could go to L.A for economic studies. Dad never denied his requests since it was the first time he asked for something for himself. He was sponsored, and then, out of boredom, he joined basketball. He got settled in, and one day, he finally felt close enough to call me and share this news of his girlfriend."

"Heather?" he guessed.

"Nah, it was some other chick," he smiled, and I moved on. "They broke up, and only after a few weeks he met Heather. I guess after that, for every small detail, he called me up."

"You miss him?" the question I was avoiding was in his mouth. He knew me better than I did myself. It was true that I missed Hades the moment he left for L.A. It was hard to let him go when he was the only person who heard my voice, but at last, none of it mattered.

"I guess. I grew up with him rather than my own mom and dad. My mother seems to be involved now, but she wasn't earlier. I am trying my very best to save Hades from those outrageous comments that I once heard," a tear slipped from my eye.

On a sudden note, his hands touched my cheek and rubbed off the tear with his thumb. "If Hades and Heather are truly in love, they will find their way back."

"You eavesdropped?" I questioned.

He pulled me in and hugged me for a comfortable space. "You, brother and sister, were simply too loud for a silent room," he said. I had another small laugh before I tightened my grip around his body and sunk into his warmth, where my eyes closed and watched the dreamy stars.

Acknowledgements

I wanted to sincerely thank my English Language teacher, Ms. Sonal Uniyal. She was a teacher that every student should deserve as she was loved by all for her famous teaching. She wasn't just a teacher teaching; she was a revolution. I never scored good marks in English, but how she fashioned an interest of mine in English like no other teacher made. I not only scored well, but because of her, I topped my essays a lot of times.

There was one more teacher who was behind the person I am today. Mrs. Manisha Badoni was a literature beast and a mother before. She changed my personality from a raging girl to a smart and independent woman. She taught me Shakespeare, and there I started having an interest in books. I developed a reading habit in my high school days due to her blessings and had always been encouraged by her to address whatever doubts I had about my career. She is the big pillar standing behind my back so I can shine in front.

I believe that Devika Sabharwal and Mehak Verma, both, deserves an appreciation as well who brought my thoughts for the cover and complex idea into fruition. I am thankful to both of them who sat with me for hours to express my imagination into their digital art.

I would like to thank my two best friends, Ilesha Rawat and Shroy Karanwal, too. If they hadn't been with me all this time supporting me, I would have still been in teenage depression and taking therapies. They are my mentors, and even though I lost my real-life Delilah, I found two of her of the same kind instead. God gave me a blessing by sending them into my life.

Kashvika Pant, what can I say about her? Whatever I say will not always be enough. She was the Kimaya of my life. The line "WE ARE BOUNDED NEITHER BY BLOOD NOR BY DESIRE YET YOUR LOVE I WANT TO HAVE TILL THE END" was actually meant for her, and I love her 3000.

Another important aspect of my life goes to Priyanshi Gairola and Urvashi Pandey, my soulmates, my neighbours, and most of all, they are no less than sisters to me. They have been there with me since my lowest, so I gotta give them the credit that I am living because of them.

My special thanks will always go to Shambhavi Gupta and Puru Vishnoi, my siblings who helped me to write this book with their constant support and encouragement. Shambhavi helped to write a lot of Hades' points of view, and she nailed it, whereas my brother took sides in front of my parents when they thought I was wasting my life.

My brother and I fought against society for the rights I deserve to have and choose.

I love him, and even though he is away from me, a part of me has always lain within him, and vice versa.

About the Book

My real-life Hades and I met through a video call from a common friend. My best friend was somehow a good friend of his, but I was too blind to notice that they all wanted to set me up with him.

I thought of him as very close to me as I shared with him about my first love.

The week that I got a proposal from my real-life Hades, was the same week I got rejected from a love I happened to have for five years. He knew, he supported, and stood by my side as a friend because he knew how inconsolable I was.

I won't lie about the fact that I promised myself never to love again, but I remember an incident very clearly in my heart when I went out with my friends, and he was there. A trend was pulled at that time of recreating an interview of Priyanka Chopra Jonas getting pulled by Nick Jonas, which I didn't know of.

He recreated it with me when I wanted to whisper a secret in his ear. I was too close to him to think of anything when I realised I had fallen in love with him.

I never wanted our friendship to be over.

I WISH HE AND I COULD RELIVE OUR FRIENDSHIP, DELETING THE PART WHERE I FELL IN LOVE WITH HIM.

Everyone in our school thought we were dating; nonetheless, they knew that we were platonic. Little did we know that just a slight misunderstanding changed the whole concept of our friendship and the tracks of our future.

He left me for another girl, and I slowly started to shut down. Not only did I lose him, but I also lost all my friends too. I had no one to rely on, but I found myself again when I met four amazing people in my life.

All my thanks go to Shroy Karanwal, Ilesha Rawat, Kashvika Pant, and Saanvi Sethi.

Know About Author

It all started with the video call. If it hadn't been for me to be bored with life and join the call for fun, I would have never met my real life, Hades. He was everything I was looking for, but yet I was still pursuing someone from my past.

This page is not about me, but it is about how it led me to make this book. The wedding scene was just something I wanted to manifest, and so did he, but with different people.

The post-breakup part isn't true either because my real-life Hades and I have never talked since. We loathed each other from within, but he was a part of my life that I never wanted to forget. I still remember him as the guy that my parents loved and cherished.

Our story was never meant to be completed in this universe, but I hope it does in another.

My real-life Delilah isn't with me anymore, and she was everything that a best friend needed to be. Just advice to my readers, if you find people you love and want to treasure, don't get yourself manipulated by people.

Hayley and Hades were in real life together and happy, and I found my happiness in writing. I never wanted to chase anyone. He was my second love and my best friend before it. Heartbroken as I was, I decided to let myself go from the capture of his thoughts and work on my career.

It was my art of letting go.

I surely wasn't the Heather of his story, and neither was he Hades for someone else, but in the present, both of us are happy enough to let go of the past and start ourselves with new beginnings.

The space between us is still there, and it is going to be until eternity.

– Shyra